A
Harlequin
Romance

OTHER
Harlequin Romances
by GWEN WESTWOOD

Many of these titles are available at your local bookseller,
or through the Harlequin Reader Service.

For a free catalogue listing all available Harlequin Romances,
send your name and address to:

HARLEQUIN READER SERVICE,
M.P.O. Box 707, Niagara Falls, N.Y. 14302
Canadian address: Stratford, Ontario, Canada.

or use coupon at back of book.

SWEET ROOTS AND HONEY

by

GWEN WESTWOOD

HARLEQUIN BOOKS

TORONTO
WINNIPEG

Original hard cover editon published in 1974
by Mills & Boon Limited.

© Gwen Westwood 1974

SBN 373-01843-6

Harlequin edition published January 1974

Printed in Canada

1843

CHAPTER ONE

'ARE you turning me out into that icy blast so soon?' Denis asked Perry.

During the short walk across the pavement from the car to the entrance of the block of flats, the cold Johannesburg winter wind had pierced through the clothes they had worn for the evening's dining and dancing, but here in the foyer the air was warm and scented with the clovelike smell of carnations from the big arrangement at the reception desk where the night porter nodded over his cowboy yarn.

'Sorry, Denis, it has been a long day and tomorrow will be worse. I still have to tie up some ends with Mike. He's catching the train tomorrow morning for that Kalahari expedition and I'm to be left in charge of the studio.'

'I suppose that means you'll have even less time for seeing me.'

'I expect I shall be busy,' Perry admitted. 'He's going to be away for at least six weeks.'

She turned her face at the last moment to avoid his kiss on her lips. With her this was an automatic gesture and, feeling rather ashamed of it, she gave him a swift soft kiss and started to walk towards the elevator.

He followed her and waited as she pressed the bell.

'I never knew anyone could look so alluring and be so sisterly. Are you never tempted to forget that cool career girl reputation?'

Perry smiled and left the question unanswered as she stepped in. As the door closed, she thought she heard Denis saying something about phoning next week.

There was a mirror in the elevator that was taking her swiftly upwards to the small penthouse on the twentieth floor of this luxury block above the city. It showed a woman, young but no longer a girl, taller than usual with a strong slender figure. Tawny eyes gazed gravely from the oval face with its creamy skin and level mouth, but the startling feature in the mirror was the long beautiful hair that hung in a fall of shining chestnut giving off sparks of bright fire even in this dim light.

She breathed a sigh of relief as she unlocked the door of her apartment. The large room with its gold and cream furnishings seemed to welcome her and thankfully she changed into a warm dark green velvet housegown and strolled into the small neat kitchen to make herself some hot chocolate.

She felt restless and somehow dissatisfied tonight. She thought briefly of the past evening. It had been pleasant enought. Denis was her current escort on the Johannesburg scene, agreeable, well-dressed and an amusing companion and like most young men in Johannesburg obsessed with making money. He seemed to Perry to be one of a long succession of men who had shown interest in her since she had made a success of her career in photography. Over and over again she met the same kind of person from the advertising world.

But why did she seem to attract men who seemed to require someone stronger-minded than themselves? She supposed it was because she was an independent type herself and invariably made it clear that she was not interested in romance or marriage, so therefore she attracted young men who wanted to steer clear of entanglements but were grateful to find a woman who looked well to take about and who ran a small car and did not expect expensive presents and was always willing to pay her share but liked to go to glamorous places for dining out.

Inside the flat the air was warm and still faintly fragrant with the scent she had used before going out, an expensive one that was co-ordinated with her bath essence, talc and cologne. It was made in Paris and had a flowerlike yet sophisticated quality.

Sipping the hot chocolate, she sat curled up on the deep cushions of the tweedy cream settee that was placed so that she could look out upon the wonderful view seen through the plate-glass window. The thousand lights of the city of gold sparkled and twinkled in the bright cold air. The room was warmed by the air-conditioner that gave her coolness in summer, but tonight she regretted even the mock log heater that she had discarded when she had been able to afford this more sophisticated method of heating. She could not remember when she had last sat in front of a real fire. Doubtless Mike would be getting plenty of experience of that kind of thing when he set out on his expedition tomorrow.

'Men have all the luck,' she had grumbled. 'I'd give anything to go on an expedition like that, deep into the heart of the desert to photograph game and Bushmen.'

'As a matter of fact,' Mike had said, 'there is a woman coming. My wife wasn't too pleased when she heard about it, but I assured her I wasn't interested in spoiled young rich girls.'

'I didn't know that Fabian Sinclair ever took women on these expeditions. I'd imagined it was an all-man affair.'

'They usually are. But this time he's been persuaded to take Paul Curtis along – you know, the well-known television personality, and his daughter, Samantha. My guess is that they're paying a large sum for the privilege

7

of joining Fabian. And he needs the money to finance the expedition. He's certainly not keen to take women on this kind of jaunt. Anyhow, Perry love, I need you to hold the fort while I'm gone and to keep an eye on Faith as well. You know she's expecting a baby and hasn't been awfully well. But I'll only be away for six weeks.'

Perry envied Mike his opportunity and yet she thought to herself she could not have joined this particular expedition. She had not told Mike, for he was so full of admiration for its leader, Fabian Sinclair, but although he did not know it and in fact she had never met him, it was he, this well-known wild life personality, who was the cause of her feeling of dissatisfaction almost amounting to despondency that she was experiencing in her life in Johannesburg.

She was aroused from these thoughts by a sudden sharp knock on the door. Whoever could this be? In Johannesburg one did not open one's door after dark and it was almost midnight. There was a heavy chain upon it, but first Perry applied her eye to the small round peephole let into the wood. Eerie and disembodied, the face of Mike swam into her vision and she quickly undid the chain.

'Mike, what are you doing here at this hour? Whatever's wrong?'

'It's Faith. I've had to take her to hospital with a threatened miscarriage. I can't leave her like this. Perry, you'll have to take my place.'

'Me? But, Mike, you must be crazy! How can I?'

Mike sat down on the couch and put his head in his hands. 'I couldn't get you on the phone. I'm just about all in. I've been at the hospital for three hours. She was ill and all alone when I got home and I had to get the doctor and then rush her in. Poor Faith, one moment

8

she was telling me I must go and then she would implore me to stay. She's so fragile, Perry. I was mad to think I could leave her for six weeks. The logical solution is that you should go. You know you've always said you would love it.'

'Yes, but Mike...'

'I've thought about it. It's no use trying to get anyone else at this late hour. You're the only one who understands the complicated foreign camera we use. If you're thinking you haven't the right clothes, you won't need much, and when you join Fabian in Mafeking you'll be able to take his advice and get anything you need before flying on in the chartered plane.'

Fabian Sinclair. For the moment she had forgotten this complication.

'Mike, I'm dreadfully sorry. You know I'd do anything to help, anything within my power. But this is impossible. I can't do it.'

Mike's eyes were shadowed. He looked ten years older since she had seen him this afternoon.

'But, Perry, I don't understand. I thought you would jump at the chance, even if it is at the last minute. I thought I could rely on you.'

Perry walked towards the window. What was she to do?

'I can't go with Fabian Sinclair. Please don't ask me.'

'But I don't get this. What have you against Fabian? I didn't know you'd ever met him.'

'I haven't.'

'Then why? Oh, for heaven's sake, Perry! His reputation as a Casanova has been exaggerated. He isn't so interested in women, especially when he's on an expedition. It's only when he's relaxing in civilization that he, shall we say, enjoys women's company. On a trip of

9

this nature he wouldn't care if you were a robot, so long as you were a robot who could take photographs superbly . . . and you can.'

'It isn't that at all. At least, it's just that long ago, about eight years, in fact, he did something that affected my life very badly, or so I thought.'

'Good God, Perry, this isn't like you, to hold a grudge against a man you've never met for some imagined slight. Well, I can tell you he doesn't have any feeling of this nature against you. He welcomed the suggestion that you should substitute for me quite agreeably if not with wild enthusiasm.'

'What? You told him I would come?'

'I was desperate. I phoned to suggest you should come. The line was bad, but he assured me that I mustn't leave Faith and that he was quite prepared that you should join his expedition if I could vouch for your skill in photography.'

Perry walked backwards and forwards like a restless lioness, shaking the mane of her bright hair.

'Mike, I just don't know what to say. I'd do anything for you but this . . .'

Mike wore a puzzled frown.

'I'm sorry if I've upset you. You were the least of my worries. You've always seemed like a tower of strength to me. That's why, when I was going, I didn't mind the idea of leaving Faith. I knew you'd keep an eye on her. God knows what I'm to do. I should phone the hospital now. Do you mind?'

'No, of course not. Go ahead.'

Perry paced across to the window as Mike dialled the number. What a dilemma! But perhaps Mike was exaggerating Faith's illness. She thought briefly but without bitterness how Mike was the only man who had interested her since her ill-fated love affair when she was eighteen. Although there was nothing thrilling or romantic in their association, they seemed to have so much in common, and she was just beginning to wonder whether it would lead to marriage when her mother wrote to ask her if she would put up an old school friend in her flat, while she found her feet in her new job in Johannesburg.

'You remember Faith,' she had written. 'Her mother is worried about her coming to a big city because she's always been so helpless.'

So she had come, and Perry had taken her under her wing, introduced her to her friends and, with her large blue eyes and fragile delicate prettiness, she had found plenty of men attracted to her. But it was Mike who had been completely bowled over from the start, Mike, who had always vowed he liked independent women who were competent and talented. And so Perry had disguised her hurt and been bridesmaid at the wedding and had promised to care for Faith during the six weeks when Mike was to be away. But with her illness the situation had changed.

She gazed unseeingly at the dark blue sky and the outline of the mine dumps in the distance. I simply can't do it, she thought. I disliked the idea of him so much in those days long ago. It would bring all the useless wasted heartbreak back again if I were to meet him. It was he who advised Mark that he shouldn't marry me. How can I be unaffected by something that seemed to alter my whole existence at the time?

Mike put the receiver down and she came to herself.

'What news?'

His colour was ashen. 'She's very ill. I must go, Perry. I feel completely at sea. I don't know which way to turn. I never dreamed you would object to going in my place.

I thought you'd jump at it.'

I can't do this to him. I'm just being selfish. Mike is probably right. How can a thing that happened eight years ago be allowed to interfere with the present?

Before she had time to regret it she held out her hand and said, 'Don't worry any more, Mike. Of course I'll go. I guess I was being childish. I'm a big girl now. Tell me what I must take and what arrangements you've made.'

Mike breathed a gusty sigh of relief.

'I was leaving on the evening train. You'll have the morning to get some togs for yourself. But not too much. It's best to travel light.'

That she was certainly doing, she reflected as she tried in vain to settle down to sleep on the hard couch in the train compartment that was bearing her inexorably through the black night. On the rack there was one small twenty-four-inch suitcase. That was all she was taking besides the considerable bulk of her photographic equipment. The arrangement was that she was to travel by train to a town on the border and be flown by private plane to meet the other members of the party who had assembled at a small village on the edge of the desert. She was to be met by Fabian Sinclair on the station and fly with him in a small twin-engined plane.

'You must be mad . . . you must be mad . . . you must be mad . . .' the turning wheels of the train told her as it raced forward in to the blackness of an African night . . . 'What have you done . . . what have you done . . . what have you done . . .' If she was to face up to meeting this man she had always considered as her enemy, she must think things over calmly and bring herself to some kind of calmness. Otherwise the situation would be impossible. She cast her mind back to the past and the incidents that had made her the cool careful person she now was.

There was nothing very dramatic about it. When she was seventeen, she had gone with a school expedition to a mountain reserve and had there met a young student with whom she had fallen in love deeply and, she thought, finally. She had always been a reserved young girl, orphaned very young and brought up by different relatives who handed her around from one to the other and were rich but not very demonstrative. She had spent most of her time at boarding school and this sudden affection and warmth she felt for Mark Winthrop was a revelation to her. He confided to her that he hoped to make a career as a wild life expert when he had finished his science degree. He was at the University of the Witwatersrand in Johannesburg and they were able to meet sometimes when the opportunity arose.

Their love for each other made him impatient of studying and one day he told her he had made up his mind to ask Fabian Sinclair for a job so that they could marry. Already Perry had heard of Fabian, who was making his name as an authority on African wild life, and she was glad and eager that he should be consulted. At that time she had no other idea in her head but the desire to marry Mark, make a home for him and bear his children. She did not want to think of any other way of life. She, who had always been used to every luxury, was quite prepared to live in poverty if they could only marry.

It was an appalling shock therefore when Mark came back to her after the interview with Fabian to find that the older man had succeeded in persuading him to change his ideas.

'He says it's useless to hope to get ahead without some kind of proper qualification.'

'But, darling Mark, you could study after we've married.'

The young boy took her eager arms away from himself.

'Don't make it harder still for me, Perry. You know I love you, but there's sense in what Fabian says. You have never been used to a difficult life and it would be hard living out in the wilds with not much money. I can't make you face that.'

'But I want to face it. I can endure anything so long as we have each other.'

Mark shook his head.

'Fabian says it's madness to marry so soon, especially in this kind of career.'

Perry tossel her red-gold mane and stamped her foot childishly.

'Fabian . . . Fabian . . . I wish you'd never heard of the man! You think more of him than me, that's certain.'

'Now, Perry, you know that isn't true. But he has made me see that it's only sensible to wait for a few years.'

'A few years!' He might as well have said a lifetime. Her flashing redheaded temper increased. 'Very well. If you think this Fabian's advice is so wonderful, take it, but don't expect me to wait for you!'

And so after more bitter scenes they had parted, and for the rest of her life up to now she had been extremely cautious about giving her love in the swift warm-hearted fashion she had known when she met Mark. She had become cool, reserved, and she had discovered a flair for photography that had led her to an interesting career. A relative had died, leaving her a certain amount of money. It was ironical that if she had had it when she was younger she need not have lost Mark. Now she used it together with her earnings to live in a luxurious fashion, spending lavishly on beautiful furniture and clothes. But her heart remained empty.

She recognized Fabian at once when she saw him on the station, for she had seen films and photographs of him and he was often featured in magazine articles. But of course he did not know her. She took her time instructing the porter on the loading of her equipment, but every few seconds stole a glance in his direction. Even here, in these ordinary surroundings and not glamorized by the photographers, he had a distinctive appearance. His height and his broad shoulders made him stand out above the crowded throng on the station platform and his finely shaped dark head turned this way and that as he searched amongst the descending passengers. At last she relented and went slowly towards him, extending her hand.

'Mr. Sinclair? I'm Perry Maitland.'

The grey eyes that looked down into hers showed a startled amazement and a swift frown marred the handsome features.

'But there must be some mistake.'

'What do you mean? Mike gave me to understand that he'd phoned you and that you knew of the change of plan.'

She spoke more sharply than she had intended, for she had dreaded meeting this man and was now annoyed and confused by the haughty displeasure in those icy grey eyes.

'He didn't tell me he was sending a woman.'

So that was it! Somehow in the confusion and owing to the bad line Fabian had not understood that Mike's partner was female.

'I hadn't the slightest idea that Mike's partner was a woman. And your name ... Perry ... could belong to either sex. But Mike must have been mad to think I would consent to take a woman into the Kalahari.'

'But I understood that there was a woman in the party already.'

'Samantha, yes. That couldn't be avoided, unfortunately. But this . . . to come as a working member of my party, having to take risks . . . what was Mike thinking of?'

Perry tilted her face towards him. She was above average height, but he seemed to tower over her.

'He wasn't thinking straight, I suppose. He was desperate because his wife was ill and he chose the most sensible solution. Don't consider for a moment, Mr. Sinclair, that I wanted to come. I did this for Mike because he didn't want to let you down and I was the only person who understood this complicated equipment. Besides, I'm used to taking photographs in difficult situations.'

He looked her up and down and for the first time seemed to take in her appearance, her slender strength, her flashing gold eyes like those of an angry lioness, and the mane of her bright red-gold hair. She turned to the porter who was hovering near to them.

'Do you intend to keep me here all day, Mr. Sinclair? A train journey isn't the most restful way to spend the night, and, if you don't mind, I would like to go somewhere to have a wash. In fact I'd love a bath. And please don't tell me there won't be things like baths in the Kalahari, because we aren't there yet, and while civilized living is still available I intend to make the most of it.'

He grinned suddenly and his whole face was transformed. Now she could understand that the stories of his undoubted charm on television programmes had not been exaggerated.

'I can see you have plenty of spirit,' he said. 'And you'll need it if you join my expedition. Now let's get back to the hotel. I still have the use of my room there, though I was hoping to fly to Ganza immediately you arrived. But we can go back there and I can give you some idea of the kind of thing you're letting yourself in for. And we'll look at your equipment.' He glanced at her small cream case. 'Is this all you have in the way of personal possessions? Well, at least you seem to believe in travelling light.'

As Perry sank back on to the grey cushions of the sleek Alfa-Romeo that he had indicated when they came from the station, she felt confused and bewildered. But Fabian Sinclair had done one thing by his abrupt displeasure. He had made up her mind for her by some law of contradiction that now she was determined to be photographer for this expedition and to make a success of it.

The room into which she was shown was like any hotel room, bare of personality. If she had hoped to learn more about this man from any of his possessions that he had left around she was to be disappointed. A couple of well-worn suitcases were strapped and ready on the luggage stand. Nothing else. It was a small hotel, but there were adequate towels and a plentiful supply of hot water. After her bath Perry applied fresh make-up, carefully wiping the powder from the glass-topped dressing-table of the stark room in case he should come back. The very fact of her sex had annoyed him, so she must try not to leave any feminine traces around. When she came down he was waiting in the foyer and she gratefully ate the hot rolls and drank the coffee he had ordered.

'Now, let's have a look at this equipment,' he said. 'I'd be glad if you'd unpack that suitcase, Miss Maitland, and we'll go through it and decide what we can throw out and what else you'll need.'

'You mean you want to look at my clothes?'

'Yes, why not? Miss Maitland, please understand that I'm in charge of this expedition. It is my responsibility to see that you have everything you need, but don't take along anything that would be superfluous.'

Back in the room, he made her put out her belongings on the bed. Inwardly she seethed with indignation, but tried not to show it. Looking at the hard set of his chin and the serious expression, she felt he was still quite capable even at this stage of saying she must go back to Johannesburg. And she wanted to go on the expedition. Yes, in spite of the antipathy she felt for this man who seemed so used to having his own way, she would hate to go back to Mike and say Fabian had refused to let her take his place.

He passed over the fragile underwear without comment.

'These slacks are too thin,' he said, fingering a pair of navy trousers that she had considered quite suitable. 'Besides, you'll find the dark colour attracts the heat. We'll go to an army surplus depot and see if we can fit you out with some khaki pants and a bush jacket. You'll hardly be needing this,' he said a little scornfully, indicating a printed silk blouse.'

'I had thought if Paul Curtis were there we might have to change in the evenings sometimes.'

'If you're hoping to make an impression on Paul, forget it. He's coming with me to get away from admiring women, he told me.'

'I didn't mean that. I simply thought that after a day in the desert it would be good to have something pretty to change into.'

'Very well then, keep it, but don't run away with the idea that this is going to be a luxury trip. We may have to provide a few extras for Paul and his daughter, they're paying for them, but the rest of the party will have to put up with the bare necessities.'

In silence she repacked the silk blouse and the sandals that he had tried to make her discard. As she did so, her long gold-red silky hair swung forward and she pushed it back with impatient fingers.

'Oh, yes, and another thing . . . your hair.'

'My hair?' She stared at him with her hands still touching the soft silky coils that hung down in a shimmering wavy flow seeming almost alive on its own.

'I would advise you to have it cut before we go. You'll find it a great nuisance in the desert.'

'Cut?' she echoed.

'I assure you you'll find it much more convenient to have short hair.'

What a brute he was! No one had ever suggested such a thing to her before. It was her hair that distinguished her from other girls. It was the first thing anyone noticed about her. She was used to its being admired. She thought of it as her one vanity.

'There's a hairdresser next to the hotel. I'm sure he could accommodate you if you explained the urgency of your need.'

Was he determined, she wondered, that she should look as unglamorous as possible? Perhaps he thought she would distract the other members of the expedition.

'And how do you suggest I should have it cut? What style did you have in mind?' she asked bitterly.

But he did not seem to notice her sarcasm.

'Any way so long as it's short and neat. I know very little about women's hair-styles. You must admit that long hair is inclined to look untidy.'

Untidy! The beautiful hair that everyone admired, with its soft tendrils of curls around her forehead.

'I suppose you'd like me to have my head shaved?'

He looked surprised, even offended.

'No, of course not. Look here, don't be difficult about it. I have nothing against your hair. It's only that you yourself would find it much more comfortable if it were short in the desert heat.'

'Oh, very well,' she said. 'I'll go and have it done now.'

But here she struck a snag. The hairdresser was adamant. He held the glowing locks in his hands.

'If you gave me a thousand rand I wouldn't cut it. I'll thin it a little for you, yes?' he declared. And she was forced to agree. Fabian, she was sure, did not believe her when she told her story. After all, why should he? The hairdresser had said it had a vibrant beauty of its own, quite unique, but Fabian did not appear to notice it. There was one thing certain, Perry thought, as the small plane circled for take-off, she need have no fears that he would be – what had Mike called it? – 'a Casanova' on this trip. For he seemed to have nothing but contempt for her sex as partners on a desert expedition.

CHAPTER TWO

At dinner that night in the small hotel, Perry reflected that if anyone had told her a couple of days ago that she would find herself in this situation she would never have believed it. After the flight she had gone straight to her room and tried to catch up on the sleep she had lost the night before. She had hardly talked to Fabian in the plane, for the noise of the engine precluded conversation.

The other members of the party had already arrived, but she had not yet met them. They were all to join forces at dinner that night and tomorrow there would be an early start. Tidying up for the meal, Perry defiantly wore the coloured blouse that Fabian had tried to make her discard. She did not think she was very vain, but she was used to wearing lovely clothes that fitted well and the khaki and blue denim outfits that she had bought that morning with Fabian's supervision left much to be desired.

On the stoep of the little hotel there were wicker chairs and tables and at one of these Fabian, already seated, was talking to a younger man. They rose when Perry arrived.

'You haven't met Ken Davidson. Perry Maitland, our photographer. Ken is looking after the mechanical side of the journey. He's definitely our key man.'

Ken laughed deprecatingly but was obviously pleased to be spoken of in this way. He was a pleasant-faced young man of about twenty-five with a rough mop of curly fair hair, blue eyes and a tanned ruddy face. He looked as if he spent a lot of time in the open air and was broad-shouldered and tanned, a very practical looking man, Perry noted with approval. If she needed help with her equipment, here was someone she could consult.

Fabian was drinking whisky, but Ken had a tin of beer in front of him.

'What's your drink?' Fabian asked Perry.

'I'll have a whisky if I may,' she replied, and was rewarded with a grin from Fabian.

'I might have known it! Anyhow, you have good taste, though I've always maintained that whisky is wasted on women.'

'A Scottish uncle was responsible for directing my taste,' she said, determined not to take offence, for after all she had to face the fact that she was going to spend several weeks in the company of this man who seemed to be living in the last century as far as the emancipation of women was concerned.

There could have been no greater contrast between the three men when Paul Curtis eventually arrived. He was entirely different on the one hand from Fabian, with his striking good looks and rather ascetic face, and on the other hand from Ken, good-looking as well in his own way, but simple, almost naïve. Paul Curtis was the oldest of the three. World-weary, Perry thought, that was the word for him. But a man of immense attraction. How otherwise could he have maintained his hold on the British television public for so long?

Tall and slender, his silver hair was styled in a longish fashion and his safari suit of greenish grey material had obviously been made by a good tailor. There were deep lines etched on his handsome face, but when he smiled, as he did on being introduced to Perry, one forgot this, for his smile embraced you as if to acknowledge that you were at this moment the most charming person in his world. Yes, indeed, thought Perry, this man possessed a

22

quite dangerous charm. He ordered a pink gin, giving explicit directions to the confused barman as if he had been in a London club.

'I see you carry the James Bond touch to darkest Africa, Paul,' Fabian chaffed him, but he seemed to take this in good part. Evidently he and Fabian understood each other. When they had almost finished their drinks, Perry noticed that Ken's attention had wandered and his gaze was riveted upon someone in the doorway. Turning, she realized that this must be Samantha, the missing member of the party. She was a girl of about eighteen, carelessly lovely. Perry noticed, with a rueful smile, her flowing honey-coloured hair that reached almost to her waist and hung in rather untidy locks around her face. She wore a long cotton printed skirt and black knit halter top that showed a beautiful evenly tanned back. Ken rushed to offer her the chair next to his and she gave him the benefit of a wide-eyed gaze from eyes of almond green before sinking down and ordering a tomato juice.

'I'm on the health kick,' she said. 'I hope you've included lots and lots of lovely nutritious food in your stores, Fabian.'

Fabian looked a little baffled. Perry noticed. While the rest of the party ordered steak or roast lamb, Samantha made a great point of inquiring what vegetables were available and finding that salad was unobtainable ate a large dish of pumpkin and tinned green beans. Paul had made an attempt to obtain a wine list, but finally went to inspect the cellar of the small hotel, the cellar being merely the name for the bar shelves. Perry was a little ashamed of the fuss he made before the nice simple people who ran the hotel. She thought there was a time and a place for everything, and really Paul was acting as if he was at the Ritz.

Ken ate a large steak with relish and washed it down with another beer, but Fabian, while accepting the wine, said, 'We've made certain concessions to your tastes in packing the stores, Paul, but I hope Samantha understands that vegetables will be scarce on this trip. We intend to shoot most of our meat. Ken is an excellent shot as well as a mechanic and he and I hope to keep the pot full. There won't be room for fads and fancies in the desert.'

Samantha made a little face.

'It sounds ghastly. But I've heard those quaint little Bushmen of yours have a way of finding all kinds of things growing in the Kalahari. I'm depending on that.'

'We'll see. September is not a good growing time. It' the time of the mock rains, the little rains. It's a time o drought before the real rains come. Often in this false spring things grow only to wither up when drought overtakes them again. When anything grows too early it withers in the harsh climate of the desert. Have you ever heard the Bushman's prayer? I can't remember all of it, but when I first heard it I thought it expressed so much about their life in the Kalahari.

'I am weak from thirst and hunger,
    O Creator, let me live,
    Let me stumble on a melon,
    Let me find a nest of eggs.
    O Creator, pierce the raincloud,
    Let the food things be laid bare,
    Let my digging stick uncover
    Ant eggs hidden in the sand.
    Let me come upon a pool.
    Let me eat and drink, Creator,
    Give me that which I must have.'

Lying sleepless on the hard bed in the room of the little hotel, these words came back to Perry, but she saw, not the handsome face of Fabian, vivid in the lamplight, but the face of the young man she had loved so many years ago. So much love she had given him, so much feeling ... the kind that is cruelly intense when one is very young, and it had all been withered by the harsh climate of Fabian's disapproval. Now that she had met him she could see how it had all happened. She could sense his charm and the strong influence of his character as it must have been to a younger man.

She herself could feel the strength of his resolve if he had made up his mind about something. He was a hard man and there would be no moving him, a man who would not understand affection to another, who would travel on his own, not needing a helpmeet or companion, not needing the more sentimental side of life at all. Had he ever been in love himself? she wondered. She doubted it. He had a reputation, she had heard, for courting the company of beautiful women while he was relaxing between expeditions, but his heart, she thought, would never be touched in these casual affairs. He would choose shallow, brittle women. That was the kind to suit him. She felt sorry for anyone of any sensitivity who expected love or tenderness for him. It was just not in his make-up, she was sure of that.

It was still dark and quite cool when there was a knock on her door the next morning and a smiling African waiter presented her with a tray of hot coffee and rusks. She sipped it gratefully and bathed hurriedly, reflecting that this would probably be her last proper bath for a long time. Her equipment had been packed in the leading truck, but she checked over the camera that she had retained so that she could take photographs en route.

Her face looked a little pale, but no wonder, for the khaki safari suit was not flattering at this hour in the morning. She found a vivid amber scarf, the colour of her eyes, and tucked this into the open neck. That was an improvement.

The small town in which they had spent the night was an outpost on the edge of the desert area and it would not take long in their powerful trucks to penetrate into the desolate surrounding country. There were two large trucks with the words FABIAN SINCLAIR, KALAHARI EXPEDITION, painted on the side. Typical of the man, Perry reflected. Even in the desert, where no one would see, he must draw attention to his own importance.

A little to her surprise she had been instructed that she was to sit next to Fabian in the one truck together with the interpreter, an old Bushman called Samgau, who had lived for many years in the desert but now worked on a farm. In the other truck Paul Curtis and Ken Davidson were to take turns with the driving and Joshua, the African who had been brought as a cook and general handyman, would be there too. Samantha was supposed to be going to sit between Ken Davidson and her father, but she had other ideas. This morning she was wearing denim jeans, very faded, but of immensely fashionable cut, and a boy's cotton jersey shirt that clung alluring to her slender curved figure. Her costume might be boyish, but her walk was entirely feminine as she swayed up to Fabian and put one hand detainingly on the shoulder of his bush jacket, pouting up at him, her lips parted to show small white perfect teeth.

'I'm disappointed, Fabian. I thought you liked me. Don't make me go with Paul. We've seen enough of each other during the last few days and need a change.

26

Perry won't mind his company. Let me come with you.'

Fabian grinned, shaking his head in mock despair.

'What do I want with a minx like you in the cab?' then, as she continued to stroke his shoulder, 'Very well, you can come in our cab this morning, but please remember that I'm in charge here, and in the desert it may be important to obey instructions.'

She leaned forward and kissed his cheek.

'What a darling you are, Fabian. Of course I'll remember. I'll do anything you ask.'

So long as it agrees with what you want yourself, thought Perry wryly. The girl was a minx, as Fabian had said, spoiled, full of youthful charm and very adept at getting her own way. Perry hesitated, not knowing whether she was expected to drive in the other cab now.

'What's keeping you, Perry?' Fabian said sharply. 'Get up into the first cab. You and Samantha are both slender enough to fit in there. I must have you there to show you the type of thing I want you to photograph.'

Samantha had established herself in the window-seat and Perry was forced to sit in the middle. The seat was wide, but Samantha seemed to spread herself in a sprawling fashion over the greatest possible space and Perry found herself pressed nearer to Fabian than she would have wished if she had had any choice.

It was a land of wide spaces. At first they followed a track. It could hardly be called a road but was a flattened area that led through a countryside that seemed to be an endless plain of dry gold colour where the grass, however, turned to silver when the wind swept across it. There were small black bushes, brittle thorn trees, and here and there little forests of Mopani trees, their leaves turning in the wind, green, red and gold all at the same time. Soon the track seemed to fade out and the grass was longer. Here the trucks crashed along in a manner more like military tanks, using their lowest gears, going over bushes and smashing down small trees. As they twisted and turned to avoid obstacles, at times it felt as if they were on a ship in a violent storm.

If Samantha had thought she would be able to hold any conversation with Fabian she was wrong, thought Perry. It was all one could do to cling on to the seat and avoid being bounced up into the air. Fabian did not seem to be in the least affected by the rough ride. He drove along imperturbably as if he were driving along a motorway. At mid-morning they stopped for a breather in a small acacia forest. It was quiet in the little wood, a blessed relief after the noise of the trucks, but as they ate the sandwiches the hotel had provided and drank the tea from thermos flasks, a troupe of small chacma baboons not very much bigger than monkeys came furtively from between the trees and gazed at them from a distance with lively curiosity. Perry was enchanted.

'Do you think I should try to get a shot of them?' she asked Fabian.

'Yes, you can try. They've very quick, but fairly tame, I should think, not very afraid of humans.'

She took her camera and walked quietly after them, but each time she thought she had a perfect shot ready they would run at an incredible pace out of her range. At last she managed a few shots at long range but taken with a telephoto lens. Then she turned to retrace her steps. How confusing it was! She had thought she would be able to see the trucks, but she had walked further than she had realized. Although the country looked flat it was rather deceiving, for it had gentle slopes that one hardly noticed in a vehicle but once you started walking the hollows were deeper than one thought likely. Added to this, the trees, though small, were leafy and little more than the height of a person, so that the foliage came on a level with one's eyes.

How stupid she had been to lose sight of the trucks, thought Perry. She was not alarmed, for surely a shout would bring to notice the fact that she had done so. Yet on the other hand the last thing she wanted to do was to look as if she had done something foolish – on the very first stop too. She was bewildered about her direction now. Suppose she mistook it and went on walking away from the trucks? She paused quite motionless and listened. It was all so quiet. She could hear the little wind that was stirring the grass below her feet and rustling the leaves on the branches at her side and somewhere far away there was the call of a bird. Then close by beyond the trees she heard a piercing whistle and was relieved to see the ruddy face of Ken Davidson appearing like a lively sun.

'Are you all right, Perry? I noticed you'd been gone a long time and wondered whether you'd lost track of the way back. It's so easy in this kind of country.'

'Ken, I'm so glad to see you!' Her response to the young man's kindness was warmer than was her usual habit with a comparative stranger because she had feared Fabian's possible reaction to her foolishness.

He gave her a little squeeze. It was so brotherly that she could hardly object.

'A bit worried, were you?'

'Yes,' she admitted. 'I'll try to be more careful. I get a bit carried away when I'm trying to photograph something. Don't tell Fabian, will you?'

He smiled, his blue eyes twinkling.

'You can trust me.'

But when they returned together to the trucks, which were after all not very far away, this fact did not escape comment.

'Interested in photography, Ken?' asked Samantha slyly.

Fabian, who was waiting near the first truck, said impatiently, 'Come along, you two. We have a lot of miles to travel before we set up camp for the night. I'd hoped to be deeper into the desert by now.'

His abrupt manner, the arrogant tilt of his head, roused Perry's indignation, but she tried to calm down, realizing that she had been at fault. All the same he need not have been so extremely abrupt, like a teacher reprimanding his pupils for being late.

She took her seat in the truck, but this time Samantha had decided she preferred to sit next to Fabian, and for this small mercy Perry was thankful. She sat beside the window watching the countryside when it was not being obscured by the clouds of dust being thrust up by the huge wheels. They were out of the trees and into an area of broad plains of waving grass with the occasional thorn bush. The trucks drove a little more smoothly than before because the ground seemed harder and they progressed in and out of the almost imperceptible hollows. Sometimes they would be deeper into a round cavity then out again up on the rim with a sight of endless yellow plains rolling ahead of them. Far in the distance every now and again they could see small herds of antelopes, but they kicked up their heels in a flurry of dust when they saw the trucks and Perry was not able to photograph them.

'You'll get plenty of opportunity for that, I can promise you,' Fabian assured her when she voiced her disappointment. It was hot in the cab of the truck. Samantha had ceased her bright chatter and had curled up with her legs underneath her on the seat and her head resting against Fabian's shoulder with a scant disregard for Perry's comfort. Perry was very weary.

'You may as well try to doze off if you can too,' Fabian said to her, glancing with a rather enigmatic expression at the honey-gold head nestling against him. Samantha asleep looked very appealing, all her sophistication vanished and her head nodding on its fragile neck like a flower. Perry was exhausted, hot, dusty and thirsty, but she would never have admitted this to Fabian. She closed her eyes and felt the lurching progress of the truck calm a little as she fell into a half doze in which the various scenes since she had set out on her journey flitted through her mind. An hour later she woke feeling surprised that she had actually managed to sleep. There was a change in the tempo of the engine. It was slowing down and Fabian was exchanging words with the Bushman interpreter, Samgau.

'We've had enough for the first day's journey,' he said to Samantha as she yawned sleepily and murmured her objections to being dislodged from his shoulder. 'There's a small waterhole somewhere near here and we'll set up camp there. If we get most of our camping gear unpacked, tomorrow we can make sweeps of the desert looking for Bushmen. At this time of year they shouldn't be too far away from sources of water supply.'

'Oh, super! Will it be an oasis, all romantic and flowering in the desert?' asked Samantha.

Fabian smiled. His expression was quite brilliant and full of charm.

'You've been reading too many romantic novels,' he chaffed. 'You mustn't expect palm trees and sheiks here, you know. At this time of year you may be lucky even to be able to see the water.'

How true this was, Perry realized, when a little while later the truck came over a rise of ground and they saw a basin-shaped hollow shining silvery white in the late afternoon sun. There were trees and bushes on the further side, but Samgau pointed to a group of green reeds across the salty surface of the rock-hard ground.

'He says there's a permanent water supply there where the reeds are. In the rainy season from December to March there's a lake here. They say it looks beautiful with storks and flamingoes beside the edge of the water and lilies growing. But now is the driest time. It will do for our needs, however, and we needn't use our own supply yet.'

They climbed down rather stiffly from the trucks and soon there was enormous activity as Ken Davidson and Fabian supervised the erection of the tents.

'We won't camp too near the waterhole,' Fabian told Perry. 'I want you to get a chance to photograph any game that may possibly use it at night or in the early morning.'

While all this activity was taking place, Paul Curtis had erected a sun umbrella and was sitting in a camp chair smoking a cigar. Extraordinary man, thought Perry. He evidently intended to make the most of the fact that he was contributing towards the financing of the expedition. And Samantha had fished out a guitar from her belongings. How on earth had she persuaded Fabian to let her bring that? In the shade of a small bush, she was plucking at the strings, oblivious to the fact that everyone else was engaged in frenzied activity. Perry went to supervise the unpacking of her equipment.

The tents that were being erected looked of superb quality. Perry was astonished to see Samgau carrying a small Persian rug towards one of them. Ken, who was passing, noticed her expression and grinned.

'Nothing but the best for Paul,' he whispered. 'He

insisted that he must have some beautiful things around him on his travels. There's a separate tent for him and one for Samantha. She has a sheepskin rug, fortunately natural colour, not white. It'll be the very devil to keep the dust out of it. But I was forgetting, you'll be sleeping in there too. Fabian gave instructions for two beds to be put in it.'

'Beds?' said Perry. 'I thought we would have sleeping bags.'

'We have sleeping bags, but you three are getting the luxuries of life. Fabian ordered another folding bed at crack of dawn this morning specially for you.'

No wonder he had been difficult with her, thought Perry. She had added to his last-minute troubles over the preparations for the trip. But why had he bothered? She supposed he had thought she would expect the same treatment as Samantha. But their case was very different. She was working for the expedition and did not expect preferential treatment. She had not thought about sleeping arrangments and was rather appalled to find she would have to share Samantha's tent. However, when Samantha strolled over to view the living quarters, she looked it over and then went over to her father. Perry saw her talking to him rather emphatically and although she could not hear all she said she gathered enough to conclude that she was objecting to sharing her tent. Paul listened to her and then walked over to where Fabian was fixing up the gas cylinders for the cooking.

Now what? thought Perry. It was going to be difficult if Samantha objected to her presence in her tent, but what could she do about it? Perry adjusted her wide angle lens and walked towards the salt pan to photograph the site of their first camp. The sun was lower in the sky now and the breeze cooler. The salty surface glittered in the evening light. She heard the crunching sound of footsteps behind her and turned to see Fabian approaching.

'We've struck a little snag, I'm afraid,' he informed her abruptly. 'Samantha doesn't want to share a tent. Of course she's perfectly within her rights. As she says, it was a condition of their joining our expedition that they had tents to themselves.'

'I can sleep in the truck. I wasn't expecting any luxuries.'

'No go. Ken is sleeping in one and the Africans in the other. There's very little room anyway in either of them. But I have a small tent that I intended using for myself. You'll have to put up with that, I'm afraid.'

'But where will you sleep?'

'In the truck with Ken but preferably, when the weather is good, under the stars. It won't be the first time I've slept beside the camp fire. I'll have to keep it going to ward off lions in any case. But the tent is too small to hold a bed. There's not even room to stand and you'll have to put up with a sleeping bag.'

'I'm sorry—' Perry began tentatively.

'Don't give it a thought. I don't suppose Mike thought of all these complications when he chose to send you in his place. Don't let it worry you.'

'I won't,' said Perry sharply, irked by the reference to Mike and the mistake about her sex. Fabian looked at her quizzically. He knew very well, she thought, that he had annoyed her. But he was thinking of something else.

'Your hair is on fire in the light of the setting sun,' he said. 'Perhaps the hairdresser was right. It would have been a waste to throw away all that molten gold.'

34

CHAPTER THREE

IN the small tent, Perry had slept the sleep of complete exhaustion and woke refreshed to gaze at the dim green light around her. Her new home was so small that she could stretch an arm from her sleeping bag and raise the flap to look out. Dawn was breaking upon the horizon with a rosy red glow, and small bushes and trees showed black against this light. The rest of the landscape was grey and dim, but as she watched, some few hundred metres away, a small buck detached itself from the surrounding shadows and trotted briskly in the direction of the waterhole. The waterhole! She would dress quickly in slacks and inconspicuous khaki top and then she would go to see whether it would be possible to get photographs of animals in this early dawn light. She rose and made use of the toilet facilities that had been set up near the tents, using the water sparingly to splash her face and hands.

She had tried to walk quietly, avoiding the central part of the encampment where the ashes of last night's fire glowed like a burning rose. But, as she emerged from her little tent, camera in hand, she was startled by a tall figure rising up in front of her as if he were a genie appearing from the wisps of smoke at the fireside.

'You're an early riser, Perry,' Fabian said. 'Are you intending to go to the waterhole? If so, you can't go on your own, I'm afraid.'

She could see in the half light the glint of his teeth in his dark face as he smiled, presumably at her rebellious expression. But she was startled when he put his hand under her elbow and shook it gently.

35

'I've just persuaded Joshua to hustle with some coffee. Come and have a cup, then we'll both go together. I can't risk my chief photographer so early in the journey. Who knows? A lion or leopard may have had the same ideas as you about catching a troupe of antelope beside the water.'

His manner was pleasant though teasing and she felt herself relaxing from the tensions that his presence had brought to her before. A fresh cool wind was blowing and she was glad of the mug of sweet hot coffee and the dry rusk that Joshua brought. They drank it sitting beside the glowing embers on the sleeping bag where Fabian had spent the night. After all, it was a good thing Fabian had come with her. Perry reflected a little later, for she would never have known how to approach down wind of the waterhole making a wide detour so that they would not disturb any creatures that might have come to drink. In the next weeks Perry was to see many strange and wonderful things, but she was never to forget the thrill of the first morning when, as the day came with peach-coloured light, she saw three antelopes, their pelts a warm brown, drinking at the small pool.

'They're constantly aware of danger,' whispered Fabian as she carefully lifted the camera. 'Try to be as quiet as possible.'

But the slight click of the shutter sent them prancing away to stand immobile in the shelter of a bush. A few minutes passed. Fabian and Perry were crouching in the long grass and he was very aware of the man at her side. She glanced at him. He was as still as any other creature of the wild, his dark profile clear-cut against the morning sky, his shoulder almost touching hers, as he scanned the landscape with his field glasses. Unexpectedly his hand came down upon hers and she found it difficult to keep calm, for her instinct was to run away like the antelope they had just seen. His face brushed her hair as he whispered, 'Wildebeeste ... over there.'

Down they came to the water's edge, odd untidy-looking creatures with tousled grey manes, ungainly with their small hindquarters and larger fronts. They drank and disappeared hastily, then all that was left was a large bird gazing at himself in the water.

'Don't waste too much of your film,' Fabian advised. 'There's lots of the journey still ahead of us and I'm hoping we'll find the Bushmen soon.'

The immediate need for quiet seemed to have passed, for it was getting much lighter and no more animals were coming to drink.

'I'm rather ignorant of your plans,' Perry confessed. 'This all happened so suddenly. Mike told me something ut the expedition when he thought that he was ing himself, but not all of it.'

Fabian smiled. He seemed different this morning, ch more approachable. It was as if the desert was his ral element and now he had cast off the ties of ilization he was a happier person.

'My main aim is that I'm hoping to find a group of ushmen living in their natural surroundings. Next to the Australian aborigines, they're the most primitive of living men, almost approximating to the ancient cave dwellers, but when we've found them it's not just a question of measuring them, testing their health and so on. That's interesting, but it's been done before. No, I want to find out how they think and feel, what goes on in their minds.'

The sky was becoming lighter and Perry could see his face clearly now, very close to hers, alight with vivid interest.

'The idea of the Bushman has always intrigued me.

There's something very fascinating about a race of men and women so small that they seem like characters in some folk tale. They're little men, sturdy and well-made with heart-shaped, rather elfin faces, and they can run like the wind.'

'Have they always lived in the desert?'

'Not always. At one time the whole of the southern tip of Africa was their home. When the settlers arrived, the Bushmen didn't understand it when their water-holes were fenced off. The game became scarcer, so they raided for cattle. They were hunted in their turn and forced to retreat deeper into the desert where only themselves with their fantastic knowledge of nature could survive. They don't cultivate crops or have settled homes, nor do they have many possessions, and yet in spite of their incredibly harsh lives they're a very gentle people.'

Perry was carried away by the zest with which Fabian spoke. She could sense how he had achieved his repu-tation as an authority on the wild places of the world. In the glow of his enthusiasm she forgot for a while that she had made up her mind she could never like this man.

'How do you propose to find them?' she asked.

'We'll start today making wide sweeps of the interior. It won't be so easy, like looking for the needle in the haystack, but the thing in our favour is that it's the dry season and they should be living close to known water-holes. I'm hoping Samgau, who's a tame Bushman, that is one who has lived on a farm, will be able to help us in this.'

The camp was astir when they returned, and smells of bacon and woodsmoke and coffee filled the air. Paul Curtis, dapper and looking rather out of place in a silk dressing-gown, was emerging from the shower cubicle and, as he greeted Perry, she caught a waft of some

38

expensive after-shave lotion. He's the kind of man who would change into a dinner jacket in the jungle, she thought to herself. Ken, already dressed in khaki safari suit, was tinkering with the engine of the Land-rover. He grinned cheerfully.

'Must see that everything is in order. Today we do a bit more exploring,' he said.

His eyes wandered from Perry and riveted on to the sight of Samantha drifting out from her tent, yawning noisily and making sure that everyone noticed her. Her lovely hair was tousled and her face shiny and devoid of make-up, and in her blue and white striped dacron pyjamas she managed to look very childish and yet very alluring.

'Heavens, it feels like the middle of the night. Will we have to get up this early every day?' she demanded of nobody in particular, then seeing Fabian and Perry together, she demanded childishly, 'Where have you two been? Why didn't you tell me you were going somewhere, Fabian? I would have come with you.'

'There's always another day,' Fabian assured her good-temperedly. It was surprising, thought Perry, how amiable he could be with the girl, for really she seemed as if she were going to be very exasperating. Though perhaps she was the kind who was irritating to her own sex and not to the other, for here was Ken with a bemused expression on his face, and Fabian with his indulgent smile and Paul, her father, obviously was besotted with the minx. Oh, well, maybe she herself was too critical. Later Samantha made sure that she sat next to Fabian in the truck and Perry found herself next to Paul Curtis in the back. Ken was driving and Samgau, the tame Bushman, was perched upon the back.

It was still quite early, but already the sky was a brilliant blue over the wide plain with its low bushes, its scattered broad-crowned thorn trees and its waving dry grass, fine and golden like the hair of a lion. Fat little ground squirrels were running around near their burrows searching for food. They sat up on their hind legs to look curiously at the truck and whistled to each other softly, their tails waving. Perry would have liked to try to photograph them, but at the moment Fabian seemed to have forgotten what she was there for. His only thought seemed to be to try to find Bushmen. Every now and again they would stop and he would take out his field-glasses and scan the countryside that stretched for what seemed to be hundreds of miles to the far horizon.

Occasionally in the distance they would spy some movement, but it was very difficult to tell whether this was caused by the constant wind blowing vegetation or the swift gallop of an antelope. It was difficult to imagine that there could be other human beings in this vast lonely place. Sometimes a whirlwind of dust arose, spiralling into the air like a living thing, and it was hard not to be deceived into thinking that maybe this was what they sought. Very soon the coolness that had been left over from the night vanished as the burning rays of the sun swept swiftly over the red dusty earth, the parched yellow grass, and the small black bushes that gave little shade now they had left the larger growth near the waterhole.

As the sun rose higher it was difficult to see the landscape in the distance, for the whole desert seemed a uniform colour of yellow shimmering heat in spite of the protection afforded by their sun-glasses. The vehicle bounced and jolted over the rough ground and it was almost impossible to make any conversation, but Samantha seemed to be managing it, sitting in the front seat between Ken and Fabian. Perry could see her vivacious profile and Fabian's turned towards her occasionally in a responsive grin.

'Fantastic country!' Paul Curtis shouted at her, and she nodded her head in breathless agreement. She noticed he was looking curiously at her and she smiled at him. During a holiday overseas she had watched Paul on television and was naturally interested to find herself in such close proximity with this well-known personality. He was very handsome in a mature way, silver-grey hair, a rather leonine head. Perry had enjoyed his programmes because they featured other well-known people from all walks of life, and yet she had had some reservations about Paul himself. He was too sophisticated, she had felt, often tripping people into statements that made them look a little foolish, seeming to take a delight in pricking the ego of the self-important ones. Ah, now she remembered, she had seen him do a programme with Fabian and had hoped he would do the same with him, but he had not succeeded. However hard she wished to deny it, she had to admit that in that programme, Fabian had emerged as a man of integrity, but she qualified this by saying to herself that this only applied to his work. Paul did not deal with Fabian's private life. But was the television image the true one? Certainly it was hard to project a false image on that frank little screen.

When at last they came to a small grove of bushes in this wilderness of grass and shrub, Fabian decided to stop for a short break. Samantha seized hold of Fabian's hand and clung to him as she leaped down from the high seat.

'I think your desert is too gorgeous, Fabian, even if it is a bit scorching. When are you going to find your little men?'

Her green eyes sparkled up at him and her honey-coloured skin seemed as matt as when they had started on the long drive. Her clinging shirt revealed her lovely young figure in all its perfection and, as they reached the shade of the tree, she took off her sun helmet and her golden-brown hair fell to her waist. No man, Perry reflected, could help looking down at her with lively admiration and she was not surprised that Fabian smiled as he replied, 'I'm afraid you'll have to be patient for a while yet, minx. But I'm hopeful it won't take much longer. If only we could find some indication that they were around, it would give me a bit of hope.'

In the scant shade of the little trees they ate a few rye biscuits with cheese and had some orange drink. Fabian had explained to the party when they first set out that they must not expect to eat much during the day. He thought it best if they had their main meal in the evening. It was too hot to feel hungry now.

'Are you coming back the same way?' asked Paul when Fabian made a move to go.

'Yes, I think so. We'll follow our own tracks back. It will make it easier and quicker,' Fabian replied. 'Why do you ask?'

'Simply because I would like to spend a while in the shade. You can pick me up on the way back.'

Fabian hesitated.

'I don't like to leave you alone, Paul. If anything should go wrong, I feel you should have company.'

'What could go wrong? I can shoo away any lions that cross my path.'

Paul was smiling, the lazy charming smile that Perry had seen on television.

'I'd rather leave two of you together. Samantha?'

She pouted. 'I want to go with Fabian, Daddy. Why not let Perry stay? You'll need Samgau in case we see any Bushmen.'

Perry did not particularly want to stay alone with Paul, but there seemed to be no alternative as Fabian nodded and said, 'Good idea. I won't need Perry for photography yet. The light is too strong at this time of day.'

Perry watched them drive away with some misgiving. Paul had wanted to be alone and she felt she was encroaching on this desire. Oh, well, she could take her camera and explore the little wood while he rested. She knew more about the desert now and would not be caught a second time by the similarity of the landscape. She could easily follow her own footprints back if there should be any difficulty, for here the ground was sandy and Fabian had told her this morning how the Bushmen watched in tracking for every broken blade of grass and so on. But Paul did not let her off so easily from his company.

'Come,' he said, patting the ground beside him. 'Tell me all about yourself.'

Perry laughed. She had flung aside her sun-helmet and her dazzling hair glinted with red-gold lights in the dappled sunlight filtering through the little trees. Her clear amber eyes seemed to complement the golden colours of the desert, it occurred to Paul.

'Mr. Curtis,' then as she saw his protesting frown, 'I mean, Paul, I thought you'd come into the desert to get away from interviewing people.'

Paul grinned. He really was a very attractive-looking man, thought Perry. 'Haven't you realized, or perhaps you haven't seen my programme, that I'm possessed with an insatiable curiosity? I must know all about the people I meet and how they tick. That is, of course, interesting people.'

He looked at her in a mischievous speculating way as they sat together. From the truck he had extricated two

43

small folding seats that were close to the ground and yet remarkably comfortable. He does believe in his home comforts, Perry thought. He had placed Perry's one quite close to his and she was forced to look at his quizzical expression that held a good deal of charm.

'Tell me, what's a nice girl like you doing in a strange place like this?' he said, indicating their surroundings with a wave of his hand.

'I'm merely a substitute, and not a very popular one at that,' Perry replied.

'Oh, yes, I heard the story from Fabian. But what makes you think you're not popular? If you don't object to my saying so, you seem to have all the attributes of a highly successful member of the party. In fact you could be a winner in one of those programmes about whom you'd like to be left with on a desert island, if you see what I mean.'

'Heavens, don't say that! I'm quite sure Fabian would be horrified if you suggested he should be left on a desert island with me.'

'Fabian's not such an ogre. You have the wrong idea of him. He's highly popular with women when he has his short spells in civilization, I understand. But he's a bit preoccupied in the desert. Here he's like a man with a dream.'

'You mustn't think I want Fabian to notice me as a woman,' said Perry. She seemed to be saying more than she intended, possibly because Paul had such a persuasive manner. That would be due to his long experience of wheedling their secrets from people. But she had no intention of telling him why she disliked Fabian.

'No woman as beautiful as you can tell me that,' Paul said. 'I should have thought somebody as remarkably lovely would be used to being noticed. In fact she should regard it as a right.'

Perry shook her head. She had no idea whether she should take him seriously or not. 'I'm not interested in what any man thinks of me,' she asserted.

'Don't tell me you're one of these emancipated females . . . Women's Lib and all that.'

'Perhaps I am.'

'This is remarkably interesting.'

His keen eyes that were green, not as emerald as Samantha's but with darker hazel flecks in them, were regarding her as if she were some particularly intriguing specimen of wild bird he had found in the desert.

'Tell me, you say you're not interested in men, but surely you must have had men in love with you.'

'Some have said so.'

'And what about yourself? How many times have you been in love?'

'Paul, you're not doing your television programme now. I don't have to answer that.'

'Ah, well, I must amuse myself somehow. What if I start to tell you the story of my life?'

'That should be interesting,' Perry said with a demure smile that still held a hint of mischief.

'So . . . where shall I begin? Would you like to hear of my first wife, my second, or my third?'

'You're teasing me,' Perry accused him.

'No, it's true enough, and at the moment I'm between wives, so take care, young lady.'

Perry thought to herself that she did not need any warning.

'Samantha is my only child, the daughter of my first wife. I'm afraid she's had a rather chequered upbringing. She became a rebel at an early age, but these days I don't see any harm in that. She seems to be able to cope with life.'

Perry thought that if by coping with life Paul meant

that Samantha knew how to get her own way he was certainly right.

'I adore her,' Paul said unexpectedly. 'She's the only woman who's really meant anything to me. And I know she doesn't care a damn for me. She looks on me as a source of supply, that's all. Sad, isn't it?'

'Oh, Paul . . .' Perry felt helpless to give any comfort. She began to like him better because she suddenly felt sorry for him. Here he was with the world at his feet, highly successful in his profession, famous, popular, witty, wealthy, and his affections were bound up in that selfish little creature who thought only of herself.

'That's partly why I joined this expedition. It was the only way I could get my daughter to myself. I thought that in the desert we might get to know each other better. I was between wives and Samantha was between boy-friends, so she seized at the idea of coming with me because she was bored with London life for the moment. And of course she was interested to meet Fabian. Who wouldn't be?'

'Yes, I suppose so,' Perry said. 'But apart from that why did you want to come on this particular expedition? Why the desert?'

'Oh, you have no idea, or perhaps you can imagine it, how difficult it is to travel anywhere where one is known. People always wanting something, pressing in on you. If we'd gone to somewhere like Majorca or the South of France I would scarcely have seen Samantha at all, for she would have been seized up into the local smart set and met all the wrong type of men. Not that she isn't used to that. She's had some most disastrous love affairs already. I've had some difficult times with her, I can tell you.

'No, this was ideal. I wanted to get her right away on her own. And she seems attracted to Fabian. So if anything came of that it would give me the greatest joy. I have a great respect for the man and feel he's just the kind of fellow Samantha needs to get some control into her life. But here I am talking like a maiden aunt. Why, coming to think of it, it's quite possible that you may have similar ideas about Fabian.'

The shrewd grey-green eyes bored into Perry, but she shook her head.

'No, you can be sure, Paul, whatever your plans for Samantha, I won't interfere. Fabian has many good qualities, I'm sure, but he isn't my type.'

'I'm glad of that,' said Paul. 'You're an intriguing girl, Perry, something of a mystery with that passionate mouth that belies its own declarations that men don't interest you.'

Perry rose and reached for her camera.

'I think I'll wander into this little wood and see if there's anything to photograph,' she declared firmly.

Paul smiled.

'I know when I'm not wanted. I'll stay here. Don't lose yourself or be eaten by a strange beastie. If you need help just scream loudly and I'll coming running.'

He tilted back his chair to a more reclining angle, arranged his hat over his eyes and looked as she left him a picture of relaxation. It must be wonderful to be as self-possessed as Paul – and yet even he was vulnerable in his love for his daughter.

CHAPTER FOUR

IT was so quiet here in this little part of the Kalahari, almost eerie. The wind rustled through the grass, but there were no bird calls. Was she wasting her time looking for subjects for photography? Just as she was thinking this, she was startled by a slight movement ahead of her and, standing beside a clump of tallish thorn trees, there was a giraffe. It was such a surprising sight to Perry that she stayed motionless, which was just as well, because at one moment there did not seem to be anything there and then in the next she discerned three giraffes wonderfully camouflaged with their coats like checked brown and gold velvet against the brown and gold of the thorn trees, stretching up long mobile mouths to bite any soft shoots they could find. They were so amazing with their long necks and slanting bodies that she felt like the old lady who, when taken to the zoo and confronted by an elephant, said she did not believe it. Cautiously she advanced her camera and managed to take a good shot of them, but the sound of the shutter made them uneasy and they strolled gracefully away, trying to escape from the strange noise.

Perry's heart was beating fast with delighted excitement and she thought of going back for Paul, but decided he would not appreciate being disturbed from his rest, so she would go on with her exploration alone. The ground here was grassy but with patches of sand and there were footprints of small buck criss-crossed in the soft ground. Suddenly Perry froze. There in front of her was the imprint of a human foot, small and perfect. It must be, it could not be anyone else but one of the

Bushmen that Fabian was seeking. How wonderful it would be if she could find them. Fabian would not think it had been useless to send a woman on the expedition if this happened. She tried to follow the footprints, but found it very difficult to decipher them because there were so many tracks of animals as well and she was quite unused to this kind of task.

A little troupe of ground squirrels ran chittering away from her, then sat at a safe distance perched on their haunches. She stopped to take photographs and it took longer than she had expected to get them in the right position, for she was remembering Fabian's warning about not wasting film. Then she went back to her tracking. How she wished she could tell whether the tracks were new or old, but she was not experienced enough to know. The sand was so soft that they did not look very distinct now and often she lost them, but every now and again she was heartened to see one more clear than the rest.

At last she came to a little clump of bushes and the prints seemed to lead towards this. Softly she stepped towards it. She did not know what she was to do if she found some of these small people Fabian had described, but she was so excited that she did not feel nervous. Round the last bush now, and into a small level sandy arena. She stared at the scene.

It looked almost as if children had been at play and then had left to do something else. Beside the bushes there were three tiny grass huts, fragile little dwellings like the small tumbled nests of birds. In front of the huts were the remains of small fires, but there was nothing but grey ash and when she put her hand towards it she found it was cold. Small bones scattered the ground and a tiny broken sandal made of antelope leather hung from a stick. Perry felt like a giantess towering over the little

49

huts. She wondered whether brown eyes were watching her from some vantage point in the bushes – but no, one could tell that nobody had lived here for a while, because the whole place had an abandoned air. Feeling disappointed, she nevertheless took some photographs and then started to walk back. She must have gone further than she realized, for it seemed to take a long time and when she was only about half-way back she was startled to hear shouts. She called back and in a little while heard footsteps hastily coming towards her. Odd that Paul should be so concerned as to come for her. She would have thought he would just leave her to it.

However, it was not Paul but Fabian who came striding towards her. He looked annoyed and once more Perry felt the surge of irritation that she usually had in any encounter with him.

'Where the hell do you think you've been, Perry? The sun will have set before we get back to camp unless we make quicker progress than this. Why the devil did Paul let you wander off alone?'

'It wasn't anything to do with Paul. I decided to go and do some photography on my own. Surely, Fabian, that's what I'm here for?'

'Not by yourself. I thought you understood that when I left the two of you here. I didn't expect you to go off on your own. Paul's a careless devil. He should never have allowed it.'

Perry was so eager to tell of her discovery that she felt impatient of his bad temper. She put her hand on his arm as if to stop him and he looked surprised.

'Fabian, please listen to me. I followed some tracks of small footprints. There's a Bushman village over there.'

He looked so transformed, so thrilled, his grey eyes

50

shining with delight, that she hated to say the next words.

'I'm afraid it's abandoned. They were there, but they've gone.'

His expression changed.

'Why did you let me think . . . oh, well, forget it. We'd better go back to the party. You look tired. But Samgau and I will go to have a look at your village.'

'I'd like to come too. Please let me.'

'You'll delay us.'

'No, I'll be able to show you exactly where it is.'

She waited while he went a little distance and summoned Samgua. She was glad she had overruled him, but when she started back rather wearily on the long trail she did not know whether after all it had been a very good idea. She tried to keep up to Fabian's pace, but he and the Bushman Samgau were very quick and she was almost panting when eventually they reached the spot. And then Samgau was not at all impressed. 'He says,' Fabian informed her flatly, 'that they've been gone from here for some weeks.'

'But the footprints . . . they were fairly distinct.'

Fabian smiled with little humour. She could see that he was bitterly disappointed and trying not to show it.

'In the desert, tracks remain for a long time. There's only the wind to blow away the footprints.'

When they returned to the place where they had left the truck, Paul was sitting reading a book of modern poetry, Ken was fiddling inside the engine, but Samantha greeted them rather sulkily, though she quickly disguised it as she spoke to Fabian.

'We were getting quite nervous – thought someone had been eaten by a leopard at the very least. What kept you? Perry seems to have a knack of getting lost with one or other of our men.'

Fabian sounded a bit annoyed. But whether it was because of Samantha's remarks or a delayed anger against herself, Perry hesitated to decide.

'Perry thought she'd found a Bushman settlement. In fact she did, but it was an old one, hence the delay.'

'Oh, poor Fabian, what a disappointment! You must have been so mad to have your hopes raised and then dashed like that. How could you do it to him, Perry?'

Samantha had put her arm through Fabian's and was raising her lips poutingly and appealing towards him. Perry intercepted a frown from Ken who had emerged from the engine in time to witness this scene. Perry shrugged her shoulders. She was determined not to be riled by Samantha's cattiness, yet her usual good spirits had left her, hot, weary and disappointed as she was. She felt the rest of the party were equally tired and were putting all the blame on her for the fact that they were still out in the desert whereas by this time they had hoped to be almost back at camp and within reach of a cool sponge-down and heartening drink.

But worse was to follow. When they arrived back at the camp just as the sun was setting in a fiery haze of dusky splendour, the cook-boy, Joshua, came away from tending the stove and spoke rapidly to Samgau.

'What's all the excitement about?' asked Ken, who was the only member of party besides Fabian who was still displaying any energy. He strode over and joined in the conversation, then called to Fabian.

'Joshua says some Bushmen came to the camp about an hour ago, but when he said the white man wanted to see them, he couldn't persuade them to stay. They were afraid you would take them far away to work on a farm.'

Fabian gave an exclamation of exasperation.

'My heavens, it's just the opposite! I want to see how

they live here, not on a farm. I want to study them in their natural habitat.'

Ken shook his head sympathetically.

'It's damn hard luck, but you know they have reason to be timid because many of them have been taken to work as serfs for white or African farmers and often they never see their families again.'

'When did they go?'

'Only about half an hour ago. If we'd come just a little earlier we might have seen them. But it's too dark to track them now and in the morning they might be miles away. They can go at a terrific pace if they think they're in danger of being captured.'

It was a rather subdued group who ate their supper by the light of the hurricane lamps. Fabian was obviously brooding over this missed opportunity. Samantha was bored and, after eating a very little of the meal, she went and sat under a tree plucking at the strings of her guitar, playing the same few notes over and over again. Perry, her nerves already taut, could have screamed. Why, oh, why had she allowed herself to be persuaded to come on this expedition with this exasperating group of people? She had not even had an opportunity today for taking many photographs and tonight everyone was in a bad mood. She glanced at Fabian. I suppose he's blaming me for the fact that we missed the Bushmen, she thought. If I hadn't insisted on following that old trail . . but how could I possibly know?

They were all glad to retire early, but Perry lay wakeful in her little green tent wishing herself back in her Johannesburg penthouse far away from this uncomfortable place where everything she did seemed to be wrong.

When she woke the morning was chilly, and yet to Perry the tent seemed stifling. It was because she felt in

53

a thoroughly rebellious mood, she decided. She must get away and find a little peace. What better place than the waterhole? She could not possibly lose her way and, although Fabian had taken the precaution of accompanying her on the first day, he could hardly be expected to act as nursemaid every time she wanted to take a photograph. There seemed to be only a little game around in the desert at this time of the year, and as for lions, surely they would have heard them if they were near.

She peeped out of the tent when she had dressed. Fabian was nowhere to be seen. She thought he might have decided to sleep in one of the trucks since the night was cold. Good, she could go by herself and risk his displeasure. Anything to experience a calm still morning taking photographs, doing the work she loved and trying to get over her irritation. But she was not to get away so easily. She had just crossed the little pan when she heard someone coming with light footsteps from the direction of the camp.

'Hi, Perry, wait for me!' It was Samantha's voice. 'Where are you going? Can I come too? I've been awake for hours. I'm not used to going to bed so early.'

'Yes, you can come, if you promise to keep quiet,' Perry answered a little sharply.

She had wanted to be alone and did not really want Samantha's company, but she could hardly forbid her to come. And knowing Samantha, she would not take any notice even if she did.

'I'm beginning to tire of this trip already,' Samantha complained. 'Everyone giving orders all the time. I thought I'd be free in a beautiful desert and what do I find? Everyone is so careful and cautious, we might as well be looking out for the traffic on the M1.'

'I suppose you have to be protected in a country like this. It's very wild, remember.'

'Who cares? I thought it would be adventurous to come to the Kalahari, something to tell all my friends who boast about hitch-hiking in Turkey or travelling through India, but between my father and Fabian, I can't see much prospects of anything thrilling happening. If it wasn't that Fabian is so madly attractive, I'd ask Paul if I could go home tomorrow.'

'But we've hardly started the journey yet,' Perry protested. They were approaching the waterhole. 'I think we'd better stop talking, otherwise there'll be no animals there to photograph.'

Again Perry sat near the waterhole hidden by the bush and long grass, and Samantha kept reasonably quiet. Some reddish brown impala were drinking at the water, stopping to cast cautious glances from side to side.

'Only old impalas again,' grumbled Samantha. 'We seem to have seen hundreds of the creatures since we set out.'

'Sh! . . .' said Perry.

Two giraffes were approaching through the bushes. With their rocking-horse gait they looked like gigantic toys. They splayed their long thin legs out and bent awkwardly to drink. Perry got some good shots of them. Well, she would have plenty of photographs of giraffes if she got nothing else. Small birds were flying amongst the reeds on the water's edge and she adjusted her telescopic lens and got some good shots of them. As she looked through it preparing for another shot, she gave a start.

'What did you see?' Samantha whispered. Perry shook her head, a little bewildered. Now that she looked again she could not be certain. The brownish reeds waved in the fresh morning breeze. Had she imagined it or had she really seen the small brown face, heart-shaped with dark slanting eyes, peering at her between the grass?

'I thought I saw a face. I couldn't be sure,' she told Samantha.

'I'll go and see,' Samantha volunteered, interested at last, and, before Perry could stop her, she had gone, walking quietly in her soft moccasin-type shoes, but disturbing the flock of little yellow birds. Perry hesitated, then started packing her camera equipment so that she would be ready as soon as Samantha returned from her excursion into the bushes on the further side of the pan.

She scanned the reeds again with her binoculars in search of the little face, but if it had ever been there it had gone now. What was that? Her heart seemed to stop beating in her incredulous surprise and then started knocking so loudly against her ribs that she could hardly hear her own startled shallow breathing. For she could see a lioness quite distinctly through the power glasses, although with the naked eye it was barely discernible in the grass that was almost the same colour of tawny gold as the pelt rippling with vigorous muscle as the lioness crouched, its amber eyes fixed motionlessly on the group of impala at the water's edge. And Samantha was somewhere in that bush, creeping quietly in the same direction, quite unaware that she was in deadly danger if she got between the lioness and her prey.

What could Perry do? Should she go after her and warn her? But she could not even see her and perhaps it would be better to keep her eye on the lioness and watch her movements, then if she saw Samantha approaching too near she could make a commotion and startle the lioness before the girl got too near to the beast. How she wished now that she had heeded Fabian's advice about not going to the waterhole unless accompanied by someone who could guard them.

Then to her infinite relief she saw Samantha retracing her steps. The lioness had not even noticed her, so concentrated was she on watching her prey, and evidently they were downwind of her so she had not caught their scent. But as Samantha came within a few yards of their hiding place Perry's relief turned to dismay. Samantha crouched down beside her smiling triumphantly.

'Just look what I've found!' she said.

In her arms was a small lion cub not much bigger than a puppy.

'You must be crazy!' Perry gasped. 'Look over there!'

The lioness was still crouching, intent on the antelope.

'Oh, God!' exclaimed Samantha. 'I thought the little thing was lost. It must belong to her. What can we do?'

'It must go back before she notices it's gone.'

'I can't . . . Perry, I just can't take it back.'

'I'll come with you. You'll have to show me where you found it. The lioness will be occupied with her kill for some time, I think. There's no immediate danger.'

Perry said this in order to reassure Samantha, for she had to persuade her to come too, otherwise she would not know where to replace the cub. But she did not feel as sure of herself as she had sounded. She breathed a prayer that the lioness would remain occupied with watching the impala and started walking quietly towards the bush. But they had only advanced a few steps when with the suddenness of a clap of thunder the whole place erupted with the sounds of a lion kill. An agonized whinny was cut short followed by fierce growling. The lioness had sprung upon the antelope, bringing it down with its powerful claws and sinking her teeth into the jugular vein. Samantha, her nerves already badly shaken, let out a scream and the cub mewed in her arms. The lioness struggling with the kicking death throes of its prey sprang away and turned in the direction of the cub's call.

'Oh, God, she's seen us!' Samantha breathed.

But the lioness made a small noise as if to reassure her offspring and turned back to her task. The cub, now thoroughly aroused by its mother's voice, mewed louder.

'Give it to me,' said Perry, taking a sudden decision. 'I'll take it as far into the bush as I can. If she moves away, shout to me.'

She moved rapidly and quietly with the squirming cub, spurred on by her exasperation with Samantha and so angry that she scarcely realized how terrified she was. She had only gone a few yards when she heard Samantha's shout.

'She's coming, Perry! Put down the cub and run!'

But it was too late. She heard a crashing sound as the lion leaped through the reeds and bush surrounding the waterhole. Then it was in the open only a few yards from where she stood scarcely concealed by the sparse undergrowth, the little cub mewing in her hands.

'Stand dead still, Perry.'

It was Fabian's voice, and she did exactly as she was told. A shot rang out and the lion collapsed like a rag toy only a matter of six yards from her. In spite of the gathering heat of the day, Perry's body had turned to ice and she found herself unable to move. Fabian strode across to her. His face was dark with anger.

'What in heaven's name possessed you to take that cub? What a damn fool thing to do! If I hadn't been coming to look for you and heard Samantha's scream . . .

well, don't let's think of it.'

Perry had never done such a thing before, but she felt as if the blood were draining away from her heart and black shadows swirled in front of her vision.

'Now, for God's sake, don't faint on me. I knew I was a fool in the first place to consent to take women in this party.'

With a terrific effort of will, Perry shook off the threatening unconsciousness. Afterwards she wondered how she had managed this, but decided it must have been sheer anger rather than the bracing effect of his words.

'I'm all right,' she said. 'I've never seen anything shot dead before.'

'And I would never have shot it if it hadn't been completely necessary. Poor beast, that had to die because of your foolishness, one moment full of life and vigour and the next limp and useless. Don't be under the illusion that I enjoy killing things – I hate it.'

He scowled at her and went over to look at the lioness. The cub struggled in her arms and Perry let it go. Here was another problem. It ran to its dead mother and nuzzled her, puzzled by her lack of animation. Perry felt stricken by Fabian's condemnation. It was true, she felt, it had been her fault. She should never have let Samantha go out of her sight.

Samantha sidled up to her.

'Too bad that had to happen, Perry. You won't tell Fabian that I took the cub in the first place, will you? Be my friend. I adore him. I'd hate to be in his bad books and you don't even like him. It doesn't matter to you.'

No, it did not, thought Perry, as later she tried to eat a belated breakfast. It only injured her self-esteem to have Fabian think she was so foolish as to take a little cub from its mother and cause the mother's death. She

bitterly regretted the whole episode. She had under-
taken to care for the cub. Fabian said they could find a
home in a game reserve for it if it lived. That she was
determined it should do.

CHAPTER FIVE

PERRY was glad that next day Fabian decided to leave their present camp near the waterhole and move further into the desert. She had been kept busy feeding the little lion on dried milk and minced up meat and she had not had much time to think about the incident in which she might easily have lost her life. At the time she had quite forgotten about the original cause of the happening, the little face that she had seen or thought she had seen in the reeds near the waterhole. When she did remember it again she was afraid to mention it in case it had all been the consequence of her imagination. She thought she was unpopular enough with Fabian already without arousing his hopes about the Bushmen again only to have them dashed.

But strange to say Fabian seemed to have recovered his good spirits next morning. He was smiling as he said, 'I want you right here next to me and then I can see to it personally that you get into no more trouble.'

In spite of a certain sulkiness on Samantha's part she had to accept Fabian's command to sit in the other truck with Paul and Ken while Samgau sat on the top of Fabian's truck. From there he could survey the landscape and notice any movement in the grass and shrubs. Although it seemed a rather perilous perch, he seemed quite happy about it and was prepared to signal by knocking on the roof of the cab if he saw any sign of life.

So Perry found herself alone with Fabian and tried to tell herself that she did not care if he disapproved of her, but all the same she felt that in a way the lion episode had been her fault and she wished it had never happened. She could not feel at ease with this man. She never had done, and now it was worse. She hated to feel that she had been in the wrong and that he had been maddeningly right when he had said she should not go to the waterhole on her own. This country looked so harmless in some ways, almost like a great parkland, and yet it abounded in danger in the shape of beasts of prey and other hazards. Even as she was thinking this, Fabian said to her, 'Look ahead,' and she saw a horned viper sliding across the track, bright and beautiful as a piece of patterned tapestry but deadly in its unconscious evil. She uttered an involuntary exclamation and he turned towards her for a moment, his grey eyes bright and sparkling.

'I didn't realize there would be snakes,' Perry said before she could stop herself.

'Snakes? Oh, yes, by the thousand. I should think, in these hot dry conditions. But don't worry. They're probably quite as frightened of you as you are of them. They only attack if you get in their way and if they consider themselves in danger. They avoid an encounter if they can help it.'

His eyes were fixed on the road ahead now, but one hand came from the wheel and to Perry's astonishment and embarrassment he grasped hers firmly.

'Are you feeling better now?' he asked.

'Yes, yes, I am. Only bitterly sorry about the death of the lioness.'

His hand was warm and firm and strangely enough she did feel much better. Her spirits lifted and the depression she had felt since yesterday vanished away like the blue mist that heralded the morning.

'I was rather hasty with you, I realize that now. The lioness was old and sick – that's why it was alone. And that's why I got the Africans to bury it without skinning the carcase. It was probably a kindness to put it out of its misery. It had a clean swift death instead of a lingering one pestered by hyenas and jackals. The cub seems healthy enough.'

He said no more and his hand returned to the wheel, but Perry was amazed how happy she felt now. The high dome of the bright blue sky over the wide golden plains gave her a sense of freedom which she had never had in her life in the city.

'Have you thought of a name for the cub?'

She had wondered whether she could give it a name, but had thought the others would think she was being too sentimental.

'I suppose Simba is rather obvious for a lion,' she ventured to say.

'What about Topaz? It has a tawny look. Come to think of it, its pelt is not unlike your hair. And even at that age they have impressive golden eyes – again like you. The eyes of a lion show its every mood. Did you know that? They can express curiosity, fear, anger, enjoyment, maybe even affection.'

'I'm afraid I'm not as well acquainted with lions as you are.'

'You will be by the time this journey is over. But seriously, there's nothing quite as enchanting as a lion cub.'

'I've realized that already. Little Topaz is so fluffy and fat. It was its poor mother who had suffered, not him.'

'When he gets used to you, you'll find he's pretty mischievous too. You'll have to guard your possessions from destruction.'

Yes, she was happy this morning, thought Perry, driving along in this strange country that was only bounded by the far horizon and the wide blue depth of the sky, seeing in the distance the leap of antelopes upon the golden plain or the queer splayed rocking-horse motion of a pair of giraffes. Some gemsbok fled from their path and she was fascinated by their scimitar-like horns and the curious black and white marking on their muzzles.

'That was the beast that was confused with the unicorn by the early settlers,' Fabian informed her.

By midday the coolness left by the night had been swallowed up by the burning rays of the sun and they had to close the windows of the cab because the red dust sifted in, making conditions very uncomfortable. Perry wondered how Samgau was faring on top of the truck, but he seemed to take discomfort in his stride. Fabian had stopped every now and again when he had seen faint movements in the distance, but always it turned out to be an animal or just an old tree stump that looked like a person. The heat was scorching and it was time to stop for the noonday break, but Fabian seemed reluctant to do so.

'I've got a feeling in my bones today,' he said. 'I feel we're going to be fortunate. Do you know they say that the Bushman has a feeling that animals are near when he's hunting. I feel the same. I'm sure we'll find them soon.'

Perry thought to herself that it was difficult to see anything in the white-hot haze that had descended over the countryside. Trees and bushes seemed to swim in mid-air and waves of heat shimmered in front of them. But about half an hour later there was a frenzied knocking on the top of the truck and Fabian swung to a halt, not caring as he opened the door that the wind blew the following trail of red dust into the cab.

'People are there,' said Samgau, pointing to where the

land fell away in a slope. Fabian grabbed his glasses, but even with these it seemed difficult to make out what Samgau thought he had seen. He gave several exclamations of frustration and then said, 'Ah!' Perry looked and looked, rashly taking off her sunglasses to enable her to see better.

'There's another pair of glasses in the glove box,' said Fabian without moving his head, and she seized these and put them to her eyes. At first she could see nothing but the waving grass with the occasional black silhouette of a little tree or shrub, but all at once down on the white-hot plain, she saw a movement. It could have been the flutter of a bird.

'If anyone is there it looks a long way away,' she remarked.

'Bushman,' said Samgau. He was so convinced of his find that it was impossible not to believe him. 'Find him if walk soft.'

Meanwhile the other truck had stopped and Fabian approached it.

'We propose to walk down into the valley,' he told them, then, seeing the expression of Paul's face, 'You needn't come, Paul, nor you, Samantha. In fact the less people the better. I'll go with Samgau, but Perry should come too in case we need photographs. What do you say, Perry? It's a bit hot. Do you feel up to it?'

Perry would not have refused, whatever the conditions. But the heat was intense. She took her sunglasses and helmet and her light camera with the wide angle lens and said simply, 'I'm ready.'

'Good girl!' For once Fabian was entirely approving, smiling with suppressed excitement and obviously deeply thrilled at this longed-for turn of events.

'Of course the light is too bright for very good photographs, but this may be our only chance to get any. One never knows. They may be too timid and not allow us to have any communication with them. But I hope not.'

Fabian's expression was tense, but his grey eyes smiled as he spoke to Perry. She hoped so much that he was not to be disappointed again, for, whatever her private opinion of him might be, she realized now that in his work he was dedicated and this dream of finding wild Bushmen had been with him for a long time. But oh, how hot it was as they descended into the hollow of the plain! Corkscrews of dust whirled in the hot dry wind and penetrated to the eyes in spite of the protection of the sunglasses and Perry could feel rivulets of sweat trickling down her back beneath her thin shirt. There were a few trees here, but the fine golden grass waved in the wind.

Cunningly Samgau led them around in a way that would disguise the sound of their footsteps, for the wind was blowing towards them and it was because of this that they were able to get right up to the small figure of a man, who was so absorbed in what he was doing that he had failed to notice them. Samgau motioned to them to stand still and he approached nearer. Perry was almost afraid to breathe, for it seemed such a critical moment. The small brown man half concealed in the grass was prodding at something in the ground with a short spear, and Perry had a fleeting fear that he might be dangerous, being armed and frightened by strangers, but nothing could have been further from the truth. When he heard Samgau's greeting he got such a shock that he fell over and then started to laugh. Fabian and Perry could see the two short brown men engaged in earnest conversation and Samgau was pointing in their direction.

'Have I told you how the Bushmen greet a stranger in their own language?' asked Fabian.

'No,' said Perry, fascinated by the scene in front of her.

'They say, "Good day, I saw you from afar" and the other replies, "Good day, I have been dead, but now that you have come, I live again." '

As Samgua gestured towards them, they were alarmed to see that the other Bushman was retreating towards the grassy place where he had been before.

'Oh, no, I hope he isn't going to disappear,' said Perry.

But Fabian breathed a sigh of relief. 'He's coming to see us. He's gone to lay down his spear. It would be considered bad manners to greet a stranger while carrying weapons. I've been told this.'

Samgau came towards them beaming from ear to ear and the short slender wild man followed, smiling shyly.

'I told him you would give him tobacco,' said Samgau, and Fabian, smiling, produced from his jacket pocket a plug of strong black tobacco.

'I thought I might need this,' he informed Perry.

The wild Bushman was young, under five foot tall, with a strong brown body and slender legs. He wore a lioncloth of animal skin and his face was pointed with fine regular features, his eyes were slanting and liquid brown like an antelope's. He took the tobacco eagerly and from a little pouch that hung at his side he produced a piece of animal bone that had long since had the marrow sucked from it. Samgau produced matches and lit the makeshift pipe, for the wild man had obviously not seen such a method of producing flame before. Samgau took a puff at the pipe himself and then handed it to the younger man. The Bushman inhaled deeply and Perry wondered what would be the effect of the strong tobacco taken in this fashion. It seemed an incredible length of time before the Bushman took the pipe from his mouth and exhaled a little smoke. Fabian laughed at her expression.

'Tobacco is an enormous pleasure in life to a Bushman. He'll trade almost anything to get it.

'Tell him,' he said to Samgau, 'that we have come very far to meet him and that we would like him to show us where he lives if he will. We wish him well and would like to know more about him.'

The two brown men conversed in their strange clicking language.

'He says he will show you waterhole near where they live.'

Evidently the little Bushman wanted to be more certain of their good intentions before he would show them his present home. Fabian had to be satisfied with this offer.

'I think it would be wiser not to take any photographs yet,' he said. 'We must go very carefully, it's clear.'

The two Bushmen ran on ahead, their loping stride not in the least slowed down by the hot conditions, and Fabian walked quickly, eager to get going, seemingly unaware that Perry might be tired and hot. She was determined not to show any weakness in case Fabian should regret once more that Mike had sent a woman in his place. Certainly Fabian's enthusiasm was infectious. His grey eyes sparkled and he smiled with such charm that she almost forgot her weariness.

'This is great,' he said, putting an arm around her shoulders and squeezing her in a strong hug. 'Won't it be wonderful to take photographs of these fascinating people, Perry? Are you looking forward to it?'

'Yes, yes, I am,' she replied breathlessly, almost running in her attempts to keep up with his long strides.

When they arrived back at the truck, the young Bushman, although he had probably never seen such a vehicle before, consented to sit on the roof with Samgau and did not seem unduly alarmed at this way of transport. His name was Natamu, or at least that was what it sounded like, and he directed them for some miles across the desert, although they could see no signs of a track or any visible landmarks, until they came to a shallow pan, smaller than the one they had left with a clump of reeds where there was evidently a spring.

'He says he will bring people to see you,' Samgau informed them.

'We'll have to be satisfied with that for the time being, I suppose. I only hope they don't take fright and retreat to some other waterhole,' said Fabian.

As before Paul and Samantha rested in the shade while the others undertook the tedious work of setting up camp again, Perry, although she felt distinctly weary after the walk in those hot dry conditions, started to sort out her camera equipment in preparation for the hoped-for meeting with the others of Natamu's family. But the sun was sinking in a rosy glow that covered the whole sky and still he did not return. This was usually the best time of day in the desert. The blue smoke of the camp fires drifted lazily a few feet from the ground, for the wind had died, and with the homely glow and the smell of stew cooking, the vastness and loneliness of the landscape seemed to recede a little.

Joshua had fed the little lion cub, he informed her. She was rather surprised at this because Samantha had promised she would do so, but she supposed the heat had made her lazy, and made a mental note to entrust any feeding to Joshua in future as he seemed more reliable. He brought Topaz to the little tent and they laughed at his infantile growls and snarls. But his struggles ended abruptly when he was presented with his mixture of dried milk and glucose. Joshua had very efficiently fitted a rubber tube to a small bottle and Topaz sucked at this greedily. She was so absorbed in her task that she did not notice that Fabian had come and was standing watching the scene.

'Have you a colour film in your camera?' he asked.

'Yes, of course,' she said, surprised.

'May I use it? I think there's still enough light. I must get a shot of Topaz. You match each other very well.'

Perry felt a little self-conscious as she stood with little Topaz squirming in her arms. Fabian had a teasing mischievous smile when he was in a good mood. I suppose I should be glad he seems to have forgotten his annoyance with me, she thought.

'Look at me,' he commanded, but she bent her head over the little cub with its fluffy golden fur and its intelligent amber eyes that Fabian had said were the colour of her own.

'Charming,' said Paul, who had strolled over to admire the cub. 'What do you say now, Fabian? Isn't it better to have women in the party? They make such attractive models.'

But Fabian, having taken the photograph, had put the camera down and was speaking to Samantha, who had engaged his attention. Perry replaced Topaz in his box and went off to have a sponge down after the exertions of the day. She must admit that today Fabian had been much more pleasant to her than usual. Or was she getting used to him? The sun had almost gone now and the grass glowed orange in its last rays. Bushes and trees were silhouetted black against the brilliant western sky and a sudden breath of cool air swept away the dust and heat of the day.

Perry felt refreshed as they gathered near the fire to

70

have their sundowners before supper. This waterhole was not quite as open as the last one. There were small bushes and shrubs near at hand and it was from this direction that they suddenly heard a sound that was strange and eerie in the fast dying light.

'Listen,' said Fabian. 'Don't make a sound.'

Faintly but coming nearer there was a kind of music, a strange, unearthly, reverberating tune, rising and falling in sad sweet notes. And suddenly from between the trees the musician came towards them. It was Natamu, and in his mouth he held an instrument like a bow with one string in the middle. As he walked he struck the taut piece of gut on either side with a small stick, producing a resonant tune which seemed to come from his mouth. A little procession came behind him, an older man, a young woman carrying a small child in the fold of her leather cape and a young girl with decorations of ostrich shell beads in her hair. They all sat down rather shyly at a little distance from the fire as Fabian went to greet them with Samgau.

'Now Fabian will be happy,' said Samantha.

Sure enough, after a conversation punctuated by some laughter, Fabian came back looking pleased.

'They've moved their belongings to a place nearer to our camp,' he said, 'hence the delay in arriving. They asked if we would like to visit them tomorrow, when they will be building new huts.'

He gave them gifts of tobacco and meat and smiling happily they slipped away into the darkness.

Dinner that night was a gay affair, for they were all in good spirits because Fabian had achieved his aim. He produced a bottle of champagne, a special tin of paté and a tin of strawberries. Samantha livened up considerably in this happy atmosphere. Tonight she was wearing a long dark-green dress. It was made of cotton but looked formal and it suited the colour of her eyes and the waving honey-coloured hair. When she was in a gay mood and the centre of attention, no one could be more charming. Her wide smile flashed at Fabian as she said slyly,

'Fabian, my darling, I have a surprise for you.'

'You usually have, Samantha, what is it this time?'

'This time it's something you'll love.'

She produced a little black box, switched a button and surprising in the still night came the sounds of the musical instrument that Natamu had been playing.

'Wasn't that clever of me, Fabian? Say you're pleased.'

She was like a child in her pride at getting a recording of the Bushman tune. Fabian smiled indulgently.

'It was pretty bright of you, Samantha. I hope you'll be able to record much more in the next few days.'

'And now you must do something to please me.'

'And what may that be?'

'Let's have fun for a change. No one's sleepy tonight. I've got lots of taped dance music. Dance with me, Fabian – I know you can.'

He could not refuse her anything tonight. He was in such a delighted mood himself. The beat of the South American music Samantha chose sounded strange in these surroundings, but Samantha and Fabian managed to make their tango look quite romantic. Ken asked Perry to dance, but she shook her head. She was tired after the differing excitements of the full day. She was still smarting from a snatch of conversation she had had with Fabian a while ago.

When Samantha had gone off to fetch her taped dance music, Fabian had turned to her saying, 'And Perry, what about you? I had thought you would be there taking photographs?'

'My flash apparatus had to be charged. It was on charge but not yet ready,' she confessed.

'Better luck next time,' he said with a quizzical twist of the lips.

Evidently he had forgotten that he had told her they must be cautious. How was it that he could make her feel so cast down as if she was always in the wrong? But she must try to get over this feeling of injustice and look forward to the morrow. She tried to talk to Paul and Ken, but all the time she was conscious of the throbbing passionate music and the sight of Samantha looking up at Fabian and laughing with a happy certainty of her own ability to charm. As for Fabian, she had never seen him looking so alive or so willing to be charmed.

CHAPTER SIX

So cunningly were the Bushmen's homes hidden that the party were amongst them before they even realised it. Like the ones Perry had seen before, they were small, beehive-shaped shelters made of branches and grass, and they blended with the landscape as birds' nests become almost invisible in a tree. They had only settled there the previous day, and one woman was still busy building her hut. She had broken branches from a little tree and stuck them in the ground with the tips bound together at the top to form an arch. Now she was pushing grass between the branches to make a more secure shelter. The floors were lined with grass and the earth beneath hollowed out to accommodate the hips of the people sleeping there.

Upon branches of the small trees near the huts hung the Bushmen's few possessions, bows and arrows, beads, ornaments, digging sticks and strings of drying meat. The Bushmen all seemed occupied with their own tasks, but when Natamu saw them he spoke to the others and they came forward to meet the strangers. They were obviously as curious about Fabian and party as the latter were about them, but they took quick looks at them and then cast their eyes down as if they thought it impolite to stare. Fabian, Perry and the others were in some difficulty too in this first encounter. They wanted badly to look properly at the little people and yet they were very much afraid of stepping on the precious fragile possessions that they could see all around them on the ground, the small bone objects and pieces of ostrich egg that must have some value to the little community.

Perry looked at Fabian. What a different person from the one she had first encountered! His face was alight with interest, his smile attractive enough to charm the birds from the trees. Through the interpreter, they were introduced to the main members of the Bushmen group. Natamu had a wife Unkra with a pretty heart-shaped face, not old, and yet her brown skin was already becoming wrinkled from the sun and her face showed a network of tiny lines as she smiled in a friendly way. Two old people, a man and a woman, sat in the sun smiling too at all the excitement. They were dressed in leather capes and skirts and had skins so creased that they looked like soft discarded gloves. They, Samgau informed them, were called old Kwi and Nau.

'How old can they be?' asked Samantha. 'They look about a hundred.'

'Not quite that,' said Fabian. 'Probably in their forties.'

'Good God!' Paul exclaimed, and Perry could not help smiling at his expression, for he must be thinking of his own age and comparing his dapper good looks with the way Kwi and Nau appeared to him.

'There's a pretty girl,' said Samantha, and Perry, who had surreptitiously been making use of her small camera, turned to look. This was Nusi, an unmarried girl, with a lovely face that reminded Perry somewhat of a Burmese, heart-shaped, with fine pretty features, her springy curls decorated with white ostrich shell beads.

A few children peeped at them from the shelter of the little huts, and Unkra showed them her baby that was slung in her leather cape. He was called Nsue, Smagau said, which was the name for an ostrich egg, because his head was quite bald. Through Samgau, Fabian explained that he wanted them to live here for a while so that he could get to know more about how they lived, and they accepted this with a gentle faith in his good intentions.

That evening, Perry felt much happier than she had done the night before. She had spent the day getting to know the Bushman community, taking photographs of their varied activities, and for the first time on the expedition she felt she had really been of some use. Fabian seemed to think so too.

'Do you think you got some good shots?' he asked.

'I hope so. I developed some this afternoon and printed them. Would you like to see them?'

'What energy! Yes, of course I would.'

Ken had suggested she could use the one truck for her development and had rigged it up as a darkroom. There was very little space and Perry asked if she should bring them out into the open.

'No, I can see them very well here,' said Fabian. He seemed unconscious of the fact that he was leaning over the small table while she only had a couple of feet of space for herself. The photographs were good. She even admitted this to herself and she hoped he liked them. He turned to her with a radiant smile after contemplating a shot of Natamu's wife, Unkra, pounding seeds in a wooden bowl using a large pestle.

'Those are the seeds of the tsamma melon,' he said. 'Without the tsamma, the Bushman could hardly exist in these hot months. It contains liquid, so they rely on it both for food and water. That's a very important shot, Perry. I'm glad you got that.'

He turned to her and they were only a foot apart.

'You've done very well for the first day,' he said. 'If the rest are half as good, our expedition will have been worth while. The photographs are of immense importance. That's why I was so flapped back when Mike couldn't come. But I see he knew what he was doing when he sent you.'

His expression changed and she found it hard to tell in what way. She found it difficult to meet the gaze of those piercing brilliant eyes.

'How lovely you are, Perry,' he said softly. 'What beautiful eyes – pure topaz with flecks of green.'

His hand was under her chin and he was tilting her face to look closer into her eyes.

'Look at me,' he demanded as her lids fluttered down to cover the eyes that were attracting so much of his attention. She could not repress a slight shiver. He laughed, letting her go.

'Are you cold? Surely not. Or is it that you don't like to have your beauty admired? You're a strange girl, Perry. I'd like to know what goes on in that lovely head and what makes a girl like you so cool towards men. Oh, yes, Paul told me that you say you're not interested in men. He was most intrigued.'

'I would prefer that you didn't discuss me with Paul,' Perry said indignantly. She hated the idea that Paul had passed on details of their conversation. She had said too much to him that day.

'Why not? Beautiful women are intriguing to Paul and myself as well – especially a woman like yourself who seems to enjoy being an enigma.'

'I'm here to take photographs, not to be psycho-analysed,' said Perry sharply. 'My attitude to men is my own affair.'

But that night, lying in her small green tent that she had grown to love for its cosiness and feeling of security, she wondered whether he had been testing her. If she had given him any encouragement, she was sure he would have embraced her. He had been intrigued by her indifference, and had wanted to prove that he could attract her, she thought. She must forget that for a few moments she had longed to be held in his arms and to be kissed by those firm lips that she sensed could be most cruelly passionate.

Topaz, the little lion, usually slept in a box just outside her tent so she could hear if he needed anything in the night and feed him if he was restless. He had become very accustomed to the food she gave him, the minced tinned meat as well as the dried milk with its addition of cod liver oil and glucose. He was a bundle of baby charm, with light spots on his fur that would one day disappear. When Perry let him free to play, he would run after a rubber ball that Joshua had produced from amongst his possessions, or he would stalk the small grass birds that sometimes fluttered around the camp, then pounce upon them and growl, lashing his tail in amusing infantile rage when they flew away from him. He had become fond of Perry already and would lick at her with his tongue that was more rasping than that of a cat.

First light was just glimmering across the sky next morning when Perry heard a scuffling and rustling quite close to her tent. What could it be? She knew by now the sounds little Topaz made, but it was louder than those. At first she was quite startled, thinking that maybe something had come to attack the little cub, perhaps a jackal or wild dog, but then she heard more rustlings and subdued giggling. She opened the flap and saw the small Bushman children from the settlement. When they saw her they jumped with surprise and held their hands in front of their mouths. They were very intrigued with Topaz, but had not touched him. The dawn wind was cold and they shivered in their scanty leather skirts, so Perry beckoned them into the tent and brought Topaz in too.

There were three children, a little girl of about seven, who was carrying the baby toddler Nsue, and a boy of about ten. It was a tight squash, but these children were used to having little space in their own homes and turned around to sit down as neatly as cats, gazing at Perry and Topaz with wide-eyed amazement. She found some sweets for them and they sat carefully licking them. They laughed very sweetly when she fed Topaz with a feeding bottle. Perry was touched that these children, living in such wild conditions, were like any other children all over the world with their vivid interest in their surroundings and their gaiety and laughter. Topaz was becoming restless now, so they went out into the open air.

'I didn't realize you had some companions in your tent,' called Fabian, who always seemed to be up and ready to start the day before anyone else. 'Come and have coffee.'

The incident yesterday might never have happened, Perry reflected. She hoped she had made it clear that she was not interested in his attentions, however flattering they might be. She was certain it had been just an impulse. If he was interested in anyone it was Samantha, whose youthful charm seemed to attract him very much. The children ran back along the little track they had trodden between the camp and the settlement, and she was left alone with Fabian clutching a mug of hot coffee and trying to hide the embarrassment at meeting him again when she had thought of him so much during wakeful moments of the night. But now he was courteous and cool, telling her of his plans for the day.

'I think it might be a good idea if you came with me when I go with the women to observe how they gather food in the desert. Samgau will come too so that we can ask for information. They walk a long way during the

Grasshopper, to whom she had given sweets, came running to her and thrust something into her hand. She gazed in horror at the fat black grubs, but realized she must not drop them. Apparently it was a precious gift she had received. She understood this much more as she observed the other children stuffing the wriggling creatures eagerly into their mouths. She turned to Fabian.

'What should I do?'

He threw back his head, laughing heartily, but took the grubs away and gave them to Samgau. 'Tell them that their friend thanks them but is not hungry. She would like them cooked for her supper.'

'Oh, please, don't say that. They'll probably bring them tonight,' she implored him.

'Then I'll help you eat them. It won't be the first time I've eaten things like that. Anyhow, what about snails? You would pay a lot in a Johannesburg restaurant for such delicacies.'

Meanwhile Natamu's wife, Unkra, had found a tree with a hollow that contained a little water, for she had plucked a blade of dry grass and was drawing it up in her mouth and then feeding little Ostrich Egg as a bird feeds her young. Perry took photographs of this charming mother and baby scene and was so pleased about this that she forgot Fabian's teasing.

They had walked a long way now and the sun was almost overhead. The women decided to rest under the trees because there would not be any shade again for a long time. But Perry was still active. For one thing she really did want to photograph all the activities of the little group and for another thing she did not want to be alone with Fabian, for he had withdrawn a little way and had sought the shelter of another tree. There was only a small patch of shade there, so, when he lazily beckoned, she pretended not to notice and went on photographing the little boy Kigi who was busy chasing a lizard. But at last Fabian called to her.

'Perry, come here. You must rest for a while. I don't want to have to carry home a fainting female.'

Reluctantly she obeyed him. He had brought a tin of sliced pineapple and it was amazingly refreshing after the scorching heat of the long walk. Samgau was sent off to distribute the rest amongst the little band of women and children and to judge by their shouts it was much appreciated.

'Try to doze off,' Fabian advised, lying back and looking as comfortable on the sparsely grassed ground as if he were on a chaise-longue. Perry closed her eyes obediently, but wondered how she could be expected to sleep when she was deeply conscious that he was lying about a foot away and that for all she knew he was watching her as he sometimes did. Cautiously she fluttered her lids and tried to look underneath them. His eyes were closed. She opened hers wide and frankly stared. She must admit he was very handsome – too handsome for his own good, she thought. Hiding those dark grey eyes, his thick dark lashes lay upon the high cheekbones and his dark brown hair sprang crisply above the clear-cut line of brow. It must be wonderful to be able to look so relaxed in such uncomfortable surroundings for, although they were in the shade, a hot wind was blowing and gritty sand rose around them.

There was something sweet about the stern mouth when it was in repose, the same sweetness that she had noticed when he had spoken to the children. But she must not soften towards him just because he was looking gentle in his sleep, for when he was wide awake he was a demon of energy and could be cruelly critical. And any approach he might make to her was motivated, she was sure, by his vanity and the fact that he thought himself attractive to women.

'Will I do?'

His eyes were still closed, but a wicked smile played around his lips. Perry sat up quickly from her half-lying position, but before she could stop him he had seized her by the shoulders and pulled her down towards him until she could not avoid their mouths touching. He opened his eyes.

'So sorry,' he grinned teasingly. 'I must have been dreaming. Strange what one can get up to when one sleeps in the heat of the day.'

She pulled away from him and he regarded her expression ruefully. She hoped it was very condemning and she hoped too that he could not see how her heart was beating underneath the thin shirt she was wearing.

'Forgive me, Perry. I'd forgotten what a cold sleeping companion I had.'

'I don't believe for a moment that you were sleeping,' said Perry indignantly. 'I thought I'd been brought here to chaperon the Bushmen women. It seems to me I need one myself!'

She looked over at the little group of women and children, but if they had noticed anything they must have thought this was the normal behaviour between a man and a woman of the white race. Fabian sat up and brushed the sand from his hair.

'I'm properly awake now and I promise to be good. I shall sit two whole feet away from you and we'll have a sober anthropological discussion about the position of women in Bushman society. Would that satisfy you?'

'I expect you think it's an absolutely ideal set-up,' Perry accused him, still feeling ruffled. Why, oh, why, since she disliked this man so intensely, could his touch arouse feelings she had not experienced for years?

'Well, we haven't had much chance to study it at close quarters, but from what Samgau and Natamu have told me it does seem pretty good. The women gather the food and the men hunt. That seems to be a fair division of labour.'

'Do you think so? It seems to me that the men get all the excitement and the women get the tedious work as usual in a society where the women have to be house-wives. The men get the thrill of the hunt which lasts only for a few days. Then they can have a rest at home, while the women have to go out almost every day look-ing for other kinds of food.'

'But the men have to face danger.'

'Knowing how crazy men are, I should think they enjoy that.'

'You may be right. Samgau tells me that Bushmen are not allowed to take a wife until they've shot an animal to prove they can support her. They propose to the girl by placing their bow and quiver inside her hut, meaning, "With these weapons I will obtain food for you," If the girl consents, she lets the bow and arrow remain there all night, but if she wants to refuse she puts them out-side the hut.'

'It surprises me that she has any choice,' said Perry rather tartly.

'Yes, the Bushmen are very gentle people in some ways with surprisingly tender feelings. You may have noticed Nusi?'

'Yes, the prettiest of the young girls.'

'Exactly. And like all pretty young girls of any kind her most urgent desire is to marry. You might think she would be happy being a young girl with no re-sponsibilities, her most onerous task being to make beads of ostrich shell and gather flowers if she can find them to adorn her hair. But no, she must be married, and the man of her choice happens to be too young even by Bushman standards.'

'How do you know all this?'

He really was astonishing, she thought, to be able to pick up the local gossip so soon.

'I noticed this young man looking rather forlorn and playing a mournful song to himself and I asked Samgau what ailed him.'

'Why is he too young? I should have thought in this society if they were old enough to be in love they would be old enough to marry.'

'No. Toma, as he's called, although he's very good-looking, has a slight limp caused by an accident with an arrow when he was a child, and it's been more difficult for him to fulfil the conditions that are set before they can be recognized as an adult. They must show that they're capable of keeping a wife. Therefore they must kill a fairly large animal on their own to show they can provide food for the family. Toma has been unlucky. He has gone apart with an instructor, as the young boys do, to learn the rituals of manhood, but he has failed in his attempts to hunt an antelope on his own. His slight handicap tells against him in these harsh conditions.'

'Oh, how sad! Couldn't we help him in some way?'

Fabian shook his head firmly. 'Much better not to interfere in an affair like this. It's a family matter. Besides, isn't it better that they remain single while they're still so young? It's only sensible that Toma should learn to become a good huntsman before he marries and has a family.'

How typical of the man! How astonishing that he should still disapprove so strongly of early marriage even in the case of these young people who lived in these wild conditions. It was his disapproval that had changed her life when she was little more than a girl, so many years ago that it seemed like another lifetime. It was this that had changed her from an eager loving person to one who sheered away from too intimate a friendship with any man.

'You look very serious. Don't worry about Toma and Nusi. It will solve itself with time.'

She was saved from having to answer him because Samgau arrived accompanied by little Kigi.

'He wants to show you the tortoise he has found,' Samgau explained.

It was a prettily marked creature with a greenish shell. When Kigi put it on the ground, it remained still for some seconds and then cautiously put out its head and looked to right and left with tiny black diamond bright eyes.

'What will he do with it?' asked Perry. 'Will he keep it for a pet?'

'My goodness, no. There's no room for that kind of sentimentality when you live as close to nature as the Bushman,' said Fabian. 'Tortoises are for eating in their lives. It will make a tasty morsel for his supper and his mother will be pleased to have the shell to scoop water.'

He is so hard and practical, Perry thought. I was mistaken when I thought there was a gentle look about his mouth in repose. I must make up my mind there is no room for that kind of sentimentality in my life either.

CHAPTER SEVEN

AFTER a few days of observing and photographing the Bushman community, Perry felt as if she had known them for ever. Their lives were very basic and lacking in all the possessions thought essential for modern living, yet they were a happy, gentle race. She watched wonderingly how they shared the sparse food they gathered and she marvelled at their gaiety and the way they sang and danced so often. Even the small boys were not allowed to fight each other, but if a boy was too aggressive he was given harder tasks to use up his energy. How could they who had so little be so wise?

Every morning, when dawn was just breaking, she would hear the patter of small feet rustling through the dry grass.

'You seem to have made a hit with the children,' Fabian commented, when once more he saw her emerging from her tent followed by Topaz and the little group, Kigi, Little Grasshopper and her baby brother.

'I think it's Topaz who's the attraction,' she admitted. 'Being popular has its penalties, I find.' She ruefully showed him a little collection of goodies that the children had brought for her enjoyment. 'I don't mind nuts, but I can't get used to the idea of eating a roasted caterpillar or a fried grasshopper. I'm afraid they're disappointed in my lack of appetite.'

'Give them to me,' said Fabian.

The children watched him with dark solemn eyes as he gravely sampled the delicacies they offered. He smacked his lips appreciatively and they clapped their hands and wriggled with joy.

'Fabian, how can you?' asked Samantha, who was on her way to the ablution tent, clad in very revealing shortie pyjamas.

'Blame Perry. She's a hard taskmaster. She made me taste them.'

Samantha shuddered.

'You should try them some time. They're crisp and savoury, quite as good as some of the snacks you get handed at cocktail parties.'

'I'll take it on trust,' Samantha said.

'And you, Perry?'

'I did try an ant, a large one, I couldn't avoid it. The children were so pressing. It tasted a bit like an acid drop,' Perry confessed.

'Spare us the details so early in the day,' begged Samantha.

She strolled off lazily, swinging her sponge bag.

'I'm surprised how well Samantha has settled down to life in the desert,' Fabian remarked. 'She's been used to a much more sophisticated life, naturally, and yet she doesn't seem to miss the city. She's making a very good job of recording the Bushman music, a thing I never expected of her.'

Perry was surprised by the pang of emotion that stabbed her as he spoke of the other girl. How ridiculous that she should feel this . . . was it jealousy? Surely not. She had tried so hard to make a good professional job of the photography and hoped she was succeeding, and yet, after that first time when he had approved of her work, he had been very sparing of his praise. Of course Fabian was attracted to Samantha. Who wouldn't be? She was lovely, young and self-confident. And with Paul for father, she had the world at her feet. Did she really like life in the desert or was she trying to win Fabian's approval? She had confided to Perry once or twice that she would be glad to see the bright lights once more. If Fabian married her would she accompany him on his expeditions, or would she expect him to curtail them?

She had noticed that Ken Davidson had a very great admiration for Samantha too, but for the most part it took the form of silent adoration. Perry had seen the look on his face when Samantha was around and the way he tried to make everything as easy as possible for her, seeing that she was provided with warm water when she wanted to wash and adjusting the rather simple shower when she complained that it was not running properly. He was a very kind man, of course, and not bad-looking, but somehow Perry did not believe that Samantha could ever be interested in this 'Honest Joe' type of man. She would want someone exciting and unpredictable, more Fabian's type.

During the afternoon, Perry sat with Nusi who was making beads from ostrich shells. Baby ostriches must have remarkably strong beaks, she reflected, in order to peck their way out of the shell, because it was quite a labour for Nusi to bore holes in it. She had chopped the eggs into suitably small pieces and was now making a hole first from one side and then the other with a stick to which she had attached a nail. She twirled the stick between her hands as she worked.

'What patience,' said Samantha, who was wandering rather restlessly around the settlement.

'Women will go to endless trouble to adorn themselves,' said Fabian, joining Samantha.'If you think of it, it requires a great deal of patience to sit in a hairdresser's or beauty parlour, or have fittings at a dressmaker's.'

'Yes, but in that case, someone else is doing the beautifying and the hard work for you. All you have to do is sit,' said Samantha.

Perry took little part in the conversation because she was keen to photograph Nusi at her task and was adjusting her lens. Nusi was so pretty. No wonder Toma wanted to marry her. Perry admired her long slender hands as they skilfully manipulated the primitive tool she was using. Usually she had a gay, vivid smile, but today Perry was finding it hard to get a change from her rather sad expression. She called Samgau to ask him if he could request a smile from her subject. They had a little conversation in the queer clicking language that sounded so very odd. Finally he turned to Perry.

'Nusi say her heart is sad today because her family say if Toma not become man soon by killing beast she must marry other man who has offered for her. Is old man from other settlement who wants second wife because other wife is growing old.'

Perry determined that she would speak to Fabian again. She was sure that if they could help Toma by transporting him by truck, being with him without doing the actual shooting, he could succeed. She usually retired to her tent early, leaving Samantha talking to Fabian, Paul and Ken, but this evening she decided to wait and see if she could get a word with Fabian alone. Luck seemed to be with her when Samantha, after playing her guitar for a while, yawned noisily and declared that she was tired out after all the hard work she had been doing making records of Bushman tunes. Ken and Paul soon followed, leaving her alone with Fabian beside the fire.

'And you, Perry? Are you not tired?'

'Not particularly. Just look at all those stars!'

The air was warm and in the dazzling heavens the bigger stars hung like silver lamps, with beyond them million upon trillion of pinpoints of light receding into space.

'There's no moon tonight. The Bushmen say that on a night like this a lion has put his paw over it so that his fellows can have better hunting,' said Fabian.

The camp fire had died down a little and looked like a spent firework. The vast depth of the heavens and the myriad stars made Perry feel giddy. She lowered her head and looked at Fabian. Against the dying glow of the firelight, his rugged good looks seemed mysterious and not of the present day, as if he too belonged to some primitive time when man lived by hunting for his food and his mate. She shivered a little and to divert her thoughts recalled why she had waited to talk to him.

'Fabian, I was photographing Nusi today and she looked rather downcast. I asked Samgau to inquire why this was so and she told him that they want her to marry an old man from another family unless Toma can prove himself as a hunter very soon. She would be second wife to this old man.'

'That wouldn't worry her. They're allowed by their tradition to take two wives. Often the men like to marry two sisters because they say they'll get on well together.'

He was smiling at her. By the glow of the fire his grin was distinctly wicked.

'Don't treat it so lightly. I'm concerned about Nusi, she's so young and sweet. I don't like her to have to take second best.'

'My dear Perry, what on earth do you think we can do about it?'

'I wondered if we could help Toma by organizing a hunt. I think the reason why he hasn't succeeded in killing an animal is that in the winter season they're a bit widely distributed and there's too much ground for him to cover with that slightly injured leg of his. If we could go with him, we could take him further.'

Fabian frowned. 'I don't want to interfere at all with their way of life. And this would definitely be interference.'

'But we could tell them that we want to photograph a hunt and that Toma is the best-looking male for the purpose of our pictures.'

Fabian grinned ruefully.

'You're a very persistent woman when you've made up your mind.'

'You mean you think I'm being obstinate?'

'Yes, if you like to put it that way.'

But he was smiling and she thought she must have made some impression with her emphasis on the usefulness of this expedition in obtaining some more pictures.

'Purely theoretically, if I consent to your plan, Perry, what happens if he does succeed and later, when he hasn't got any other transport but his own two feet, he proves a poor huntsman?'

'I don't think that will happen,' said Perry. 'Once he's gained confidence, his future will be assured and Nusi will see to it that he does well.'

'If we do this, it will be against my better judgment. Toma should be allowed to work out his own future. But you're like all women, eager to see a man tied as soon as possible. I wouldn't have thought it of you, Perry. I thought you were a career girl.'

'Not in this instance. I would like to see Nusi married to the man she loves.'

'That's child's talk, Perry. This is a wild, primitive world. Whoever she marries, in a few years' time Nusi will be worn out and ugly through the conditions of living here. You can't apply your sophisticated standards to her.'

'I don't believe that,' Perry maintained firmly. 'Wherever you live, here in the desert or in the heart of a city, it must help if you marry the one you love and don't have to accept a second best.'

'You speak very vehemently, as if you've experienced something of the kind. Is that why you've never married, Perry? Did someone prevent you from marrying the man you loved? Does that account for your coldness towards men?'

Perry stood up and he rose too. In the starlight he was a dark shadow towering over her.

'Yes, if you must know, that is the reason. But I have no intention of telling you or anyone else the story of my life. It's late. I must go to bed.'

The calm silence of the starry night was suddenly shattered by a tremendous grating roar, sounding very close at hand. The sudden unexpected shock of the noise made Perry grasp the nearest object, which happened to be Fabian's arm. He laughed and, putting his other arm around her, held her close. She could not deny that she was glad of the feeling of reassurance that flowed from his strong grasp.

'What . . . what is it?' she gasped.

'Another lion. But unlike the first one we met this one has finished hunting. They usually keep quiet until they've made their kill, then roar in order to guard it.'

She laughed shakily. 'You were right, then. The lion has put his paw over the moon tonight.'

There was another mighty roar and its descending cadence seemed to silence all other life in the desert. There was no cry of a night bird, nor even the yelping 'yip yip' of a jackal. But beyond the silence there seemed to come faintly a far sea sound like the noise you hear when you put your ear to a shell.

'How odd. There's a sound now like very faint music

as if the stars were singing.'

She was still held in his arms and now she made a movement to get away from his close proximity. He tightened his grasp.

'What a perceptive creature you are, Perry. I've often heard that sound myself, but usually when I've been alone. The desert holds strange mysteries for those who can penetrate them. The stars seem to come down closer to the earth here and as you say one seems to hear a ghostly music of the spheres. And of course in some parts of the desert, the winds blow in a way that produces singing sands.'

The silver lamps of the stars and the impenetrable indigo blue of the desert sky made Perry feel as if she was in another world, another age. And this man who held her in his arms was not the enemy she had imagined. She felt herself yielding to the magic of the warm night and to feelings that she had forgotten she could experience.

There was a sudden beam of light and a clatter of footsteps as Ken descended from the truck. He must have seen them held in a close embrace silhouetted against the light of the dying fire, for in spite of the fact that Fabian had dropped his arms to his sides, Ken made things worse by a mumbled apology.

'Sorry, didn't mean to interrupt, didn't realize anyone was still up. I came to put some more branches on the fire because I heard the lion.'

'Don't bother, Ken, I'll do it.'

Perry slipped away to the tent. She felt shaken and yet glad that the scene had been interrupted. How strange that she should have been carried away by the romance of the desert atmosphere. She must take care that it did not happen again. She was most determined that she would not add herself to the number of Fabian's conquests.

She had not thought she had persuaded Fabian to help Toma, but a few days later to her surprise he told her that he had spoken to the older men about the possibility of a hunt. They were doubtful whether Toma could succeed but anxious that he should be given another chance to prove himself. One or two of the older men, the experienced ones, would go too so that if Toma failed they might go after the beast in his stead. After staying in the camp for some days, all the party were eager to join the expedition. Perry felt a little nervous for Toma's sake that so many people were coming, but it could not be helped. Samantha, slim as a reed in tight tobacco brown jeans and a pale green shirt that matched her eyes exactly, declared that she was in need of a little excitement and she hoped they met another lion.

'I hope not,' said Fabian, 'in case it's frightened the game away.'

Perry hoped not too. After her last terrifying experience near the waterhole she did not care if she never saw a lion again. Except Topaz, of course. Topaz was a lamb, but a mischievous lamb at that. She had to guard her belongings constantly from those sharp little claws and needle-sharp teeth.

Fabian turned to Perry. 'Wear the boots we bought at the Army store today. We may have to go over rough ground to take photographs. Come with me to the settlement now, because we must get shots of the Bushmen preparing arrows.'

He scarcely waited for her to join him but forged ahead with his quick eager stride and she had almost to trot to keep up with him. He turned around to her, frowning.

'We may come up against a snag because anything connected with a hunt is considered to be a man's affair and women aren't supposed to have anything to do with it.'

Perry considered this as she hurried along beside him. The sun had not yet risen, but already the air was warm. It was going to be a hot day in the desert, but they were forced to wear their heavy boots for protection against the thorns and possible snakebite, and to wear their slacks so that they would not suffer sunburn. Perry was nettled that Fabian might be proved right that it was a disadvantage to have a photographer who was a woman.

'I have an idea,' she said. 'I think it might work. Tell Samgau to tell the Bushmen I'm not truly a woman because I wear slacks and heavy boots.'

Fabian gave a shout of laughter.

'And you think they'll believe that? You are very optimistic I must say. Why, Perry even if I could only take one look into those soft golden eyes, I'd know you were a woman.'

Fortunately Samgau was able to persuade them to allow Perry to photograph the scene.

'I tell them you are the master's woman and carry only good magic,' he said.

'You look very pretty when you blush,' smiled Fabian. 'I didn't know anyone could any more.'

'It's the heat,' Perry said crossly. She turned away from him and busied herself with her camera. Really, he was becoming very difficult. She was glad that Samantha was coming today. Maybe his attentions would be diverted to her.

Old Kwi and Natamu were preparing the arrows for the hunt, sitting some way from the huts. From a horn container they poured a brown powder into a small bone bowl wedged carefully in the sand. Natamu then cut and squeezed a round white root into this and after stirring it with a stick he smeared it on to an arrowhead. Each time an arrow was treated with the poison, Natamu held it in his hand and named an animal that might be killed, then he stuck the arrow into the sand with the point upwards to dry.

'What are they doing now?' asked Perry.

'The brown powder is from some dried grubs, a certain kind of beetle larva found only at certain times in the roots of a small bush. It's amazing how they could find out about its effect in the first place. It paralyses the nerves. A small animal will die within minutes, an antelope in an hour.'

'But doesn't it poison the meat of the animal?'

'No, the Bushmen cut away the meat around the wound.'

'What are they doing now?' asked Perry.

The two men were concentrating upon some small leather discs that they were casting upon the ground and studying.

Fabian consulted Samgau.

'He says they're what I suppose you could call a kind of dice. They're supposed to show them in what direction they can find the best game.'

'Why has Toma not taken part in these preparations?'

'It's left to the older men who've had more experience. Toma must prove himself by killing an animal before he takes part in all this.'

Natamu was to go with Toma and they were ready now. They wore leather loincloths and carried their bows, a quiver full of arrows, and small leather bags slung over their shoulders. They climbed on to the truck and told Samgau in which direction they thought they should be driven. Fabian was driving and Samantha was sitting beside him with Paul on the other side. Paul's rather lethargic manner had disappeared today and she had noticed as he climbed into the truck that he had carefully packed a gun beside him.

Fabian had frowned when he had seen this, but Paul, with a lazy grin, had said, 'I'm only bringing it along in case we get a chance of a shot after your friends have finished their hunt, old boy. I won't interfere with your plans, I assure you.'

It was still quite early, but the sky was a brilliant blue, made more vivid by the golden colour of the grass. The seating arrangement had left Perry next to Ken in the back. Samantha in front was very gay, leaning against Fabian, and laughing at remarks he was making. Paul joined in too, and Perry and Ken seemed cut off from all this sociable chat. Ken, Perry thought, was looking a little tired. She realized that without making it very obvious he was on the go all the time helping to make things run smoothly in the camp. His eyes looked very blue, for his complexion was even more sunburned than it had been when they first met. He said a little awkwardly under the cover of the noise of the engine and the laughter and chatter in front of them, 'I'm sorry about the other night. Did I interrupt something?'

Perry shook her head. It was tactless, she thought, of him to mention it, but it was hard to take offence with this well-meaning young man.

'Not at all. There was nothing to it, I assure you.'

'Aren't you interested in Fabian, then? I got a different impression, when I saw — well, what I did, though I must admit I was a bit surprised.'

'Oh, Ken, of course I'm not. You misinterpreted the scene. I got a bit of a scare when I heard that lion, that's all. If Fabian has any interest in anyone on this trip, it's Samantha.'

Ken's face fell. 'That's what I was afraid of. And

99

when I saw you two together it was a pleasant surprise to me, I must say. So you don't think a guy like me has a chance?'

'I don't know, Ken. How can I say?'

'Oh, I suppose I haven't. Not a snowball's hope in hell, I should think. How can I make it with a girl like Samantha? I wish I could, though.'

'Poor Ken! Don't feel so down about it. How do you know you haven't a chance? You can never tell. Besides, we're all living here in very strange conditions. I don't see how you can judge anything by normal standards.'

Ken seemed a very optimistic young man, for he was quickly cheered by a word of sympathy.

'I suppose you're right. But I wish I could get some opportunity to show her how much I think of her. I tell you, the way I feel about Samantha I would do simply anything for her.'

After travelling for some miles in the truck, they came to a place that the Bushmen thought to be suitable for looking for game, though Perry could not see any difference from any other place in this vast desolate plain, except perhaps that there were a few more thorn trees where animals could hide. But Natamu and Toma evidently had high hopes. They got down from the truck and set about looking for signs of animals, observing every clue with great concentration – a bent straw, a hoof-print, a broken branch, seeds shaken from grass. They turned to Sangau, who told the rest of the party that they thought the more recent hoof-prints were those of gemsbok.

Fabian turned to Perry. 'I hope for the sake of your photography that they're right. I always think the gemsbok is one of the most story-book kind of animals. They have great horns that lie straight back and give the appearance of only one horn when they're in profile. You remember, I mentioned before that early settlers thought when they first saw them that they'd found the mythical unicorn.'

It was only now that Perry realized fully the implications of this hunt. She had been so eager for Toma to succeed in proving himself a man ready for marriage that she had lost sight of the fact that a beautiful animal would have to be killed. She had seen a single gemsbok before, a handsome large beige antelope striped black on its sides and white underneath. Its face had the look of a painted rocking horse with strange black and white stripes and its horns were long and straight. It was sad to think that for their hunt to succeed one of these fascinating creatures had to lose its life.

'We'll never keep up with the hunt on foot,' said Fabian. 'From now on we'll proceed slowly on the truck whilst Natamu and Toma go together. Even Toma can run much faster than any of we could.'

Perry, who had been photographing the Bushmen as they examined the signs, now had to scramble quickly back because the small brown men had decided the direction of their quarry and started to run. They had a peculiar way of running, their bodies held upright, limbs pounding along with a high lift of the knees. There was an ease about it which made them seem tireless. Driving over the difficult ground and having to slow down to avoid bushes and antbear holes, Fabian was only just able to keep up with them. For miles they kept up this tireless trot and Perry began to wonder whether the whole thing was a false alarm. She stuck close to the window, occasionally winding it down and taking a ciné of the Bushmen in motion. It was a very exciting though rough ride.

'Look, you can see the spoor now,' shouted Fabian. It

was true that now one could follow the spoor of a group of animals in the sandy earth of the desert.

'You'll notice,' said Ken, 'that the length of their stride shows they're alarmed.'

Perry had forgotten that Ken was a wild life enthusiast as well as being a practical mechanically minded man. It was strange, she thought, that Ken had the interests that Mark had had. Mark . . . it was so long since she had thought deeply about him. She wondered what he was doing now, whether he had succeeded in his career and whether he was still connected with game reserves and wild life preservation. She wondered whether Fabian would know. But she would never ask him.

Suddenly they saw the fleeing gemsbok, a group of six animals, the size of a donkey, square and compact with erect manes and sweeping black tails. They raced along with muzzles outstretched, great horns lying back and their long tails streaming in the wind. The black marks upon their faces looked like weird masks. When Natamu and Toma came near to the gemsbok, the Bushmen crouched down and started to worm their way through the grass. The buck were tired from the long chase and stood still, staring nervously and sniffing the air. By this time the Bushmen were within a few feet of them. Suddenly at a gesture from Natamu, Toma let fly his arrow, hitting the nearest gemsbok on the flank. But the animals started to run again.

'Damn it,' said Paul. 'He hasn't got him.'

'Oh, yes, he has,' Fabian replied, starting up the engine again, although the Bushmen seemed in no hurry now to follow the fleeing beasts. 'The gemsbok will gradually die. It takes a long time for the poison to take effect on such a large animal. He'll follow him and finish him off when he's near death.'

Perry shuddered. But she had little time to think over the implications of the hunt, for Fabian turned to her saying, 'How are you doing, Perry? Have you managed to get any good shots?'

'I think so . . . I hope so,' she replied.

The Bushmen had started off again and slowly Fabian moved the truck to follow. The gemsbok were tiring now and the wounded one was dropping back. It swayed on its feet, fighting for breath.

'Let's get down,' said Samantha, 'and get closer. This is exciting!'

She seemed to have none of Perry's qualms. Fabian drew the truck to a halt and they all descended. Toma had drawn his spear. The gemsbok was standing a few yards away, trembling and apparently spent. Perry had to steel herself to go on working the ciné. She concentrated upon the task and tried to exclude all other thought, tried to harden herself to the fact that this beautiful animal was close to its death. But Samantha seemed unaffected by such emotions. She drew closer to the scene, almost hypnotized as if she were watching a bullfight in Spain.

'Get back, Samantha!' shouted Fabian, who noticed for the first time how near she had come to the animal with its scimitar-like horns. But he was too late. The gemsbok tossed its head and in a last frantic effort at aggression charged straight at Samantha. She screamed, but Ken sprang between her and the sharp long horns, pushing her out of the way. He was unable to save himself. The animal's head came straight at him where he had slipped and lay unprotected on the ground and the horns pierced his leg. A shot rang out and the beast fell just as it had turned again to attack Samantha. Paul had got his chance to use the gun.

The only one who seemed unperturbed was Natamu.

He stepped forward, took his spear and cut the throat of the dead gemsbok. But Toma stood downcast. In a few moments, his success had been turned to failure by the turn of events. The others were too concerned about Ken to consider this. Blood spurted from the wound in his leg. The horn had made a large gash and swift first aid was necessary if he was not to bleed to death.

Fabian applied a tourniquet.

'We'll have to get him out of the desert as soon as possible,' he said.

CHAPTER EIGHT

'I HAD a premonition about this hunt,' said Fabian. He and Perry were sitting in the truck where Ken was resting. Having been given a pain-killing injection, he was in a deep sleep.

'I've managed to get in touch by radio with a small village where there's an air-strip on the edge of the desert. I asked them to charter a plane, because we must get Ken to hospital. That wound in his leg looks pretty nasty. I wouldn't like to tend it in desert conditions.'

Perry felt very gloomy. Again disaster had struck and again she felt it was mainly her fault. Fabian had not wanted to have anything to do with the hunt, but she had been so eager to help Toma and Nusi that she had overridden his objections. And now see what had happened. Ken, the virtually indispensable Ken, was so badly hurt that he would have to be flown out, and Toma, she knew, was bitterly disappointed that he had come so near to succeeding in killing the gemsbok and at the last moment had been thwarted. But what a gentle, philosophical people they were. There seemed to be no resentment, only a calm acceptance that that was the way events had worked out, and a general rejoicing that they had got meat even if Toma had failed.

'What did Natamu say about the hunt?' asked Perry. 'I suppose they wouldn't count it that Toma had killed the animal? It was nearly dead, wasn't it?'

Fabian laughed a little grimly.

'I'm afraid they think that Toma has some unlucky streak working against him. I doubt whether Nusi will be allowed to marry him now. I hate to say I told you so,

Perry, but we should never have interfered.'

'And Ken? How can we manage without him?'

'I've asked if they can send a substitute. We will hear when we get to the air-strip whether they've succeeded in finding someone who can come at short notice.'

'We?' she queried.

'I'm going to drive Ken there and I'm taking you with me. I think in a situation like this you may be more practical than Samantha. In any case Paul would never hear of her coming on such a trip. I hope you don't mind, Perry. It's not going to be easy. If we start early we should be there in the late afternoon.'

'Of course I don't mind,' said Perry. What else could she say? She felt responsible for Ken's mishap in a way, and she had come to like him. She was very worried in case the wound should become septic, but Fabian had given him antibiotics, so they must hope for the best.

'What happened about the film? Did you manage to get anything?'

Perry sighed. 'It's all right, I think, as far as it goes. But of course it's incomplete, which is very frustrating. Possibly we could use it for stills.'

She had thought Fabian might make some remark about this that would cast her down still further, but he shrugged and said, 'It can't be helped. Maybe we'll have some other opportunity. It's a great pity, because it was all going so well. Still, I could hardly blame Paul. He was more concerned for Samantha than Ken, of course. But why the devil did this have to happen? Another few seconds and Toma would have killed the beast. I suppose he was a bit slow off the mark too because he's inexperienced.'

No word of blame for Samantha, Perry noticed. And really it had been all her fault. If she had not become so excited about the kill . . . oh, well, what was the use of looking back? The thing had happened. They must make the best of it and try to get Ken to the air-strip without any further mishap. Fabian had come up to her without her noticing it and she felt his hands on her shoulders and then around her waist. He drew her up gently and held her, looking down into her face with grey eyes that were not hard or scornful as she had expected.

'You look all in. Get to bed now, Perry. You've had a tough day, and tomorrow won't be easy.'

'But what about you? And who will look after Ken?'

'Joshua will help me through the night and if I need him I can always get Paul. I'll manage to snatch a bit of sleep because Ken is quite relaxed now. Go on, get to bed. For once in your life, young woman, do as I tell you!'

He squeezed her shoulder, but it was a brotherly gesture. It could have been Ken. She was exhausted, she realized this now, and once in the little green tent lay in in her sleeping bag trying to relax. But the scenes of the hunt kept pressing into her consciousness and it was quite a while before she fell into a troubled sleep. It seemed no time at all before she was aroused by Joshua bringing her a cup of coffee. Half asleep, she stumbled out to wash and change into her khaki slacks and bush shirt. What would she need to take? They would be staying in the hotel overnight, Fabian had said. It was a tiny hotel, merely there because of the air-strip and the small settlement around it, but she would take a change of clothing in case she needed it, the dark blue slacks that were not very suitable for the desert and the gay shirt that Fabian had tried to persuade her to discard.

She had given Joshua instructions about feeding

Topaz. He seemed to be thriving, growing fatter and cheekier by the day. She did not think she need worry on his account. It was long before dawn and the stars had not yet vanished. The planet Jupiter was lying in the heavens like a huge glowworm.

'They call that "Dawn's Heart",' a voice said behind her. Fabian must have noticed that her eyes were on the sky. She shivered a little in the cool dawn wind that she imagined blowing for miles and miles across the desert plains.

'Come to the fire – I've kept it going. Ken has taken a little dried milk. I can't persuade him to eat, but that doesn't matter. As long as we can get him to the plane he'll soon have some expert care. I'm afraid the journey will be very trying and hot. We can't avoid that, but Ken is a tough young man. He says himself it was far better that he was hurt rather than Samantha.'

'I suppose so,' Perry replied a little bleakly. Far better that no one had been hurt at all, she thought.

Ken was still very drowsy. They had put a mattress behind the front seat and managed to make him as comfortable as possible.

'I'm sorry to be such a nuisance, Fabian,' he murmured weakly.

'Think nothing of it, old chap. We'll have you there as soon as we can make it and the plane will do the rest. In no time at all you'll be able to rejoin us.'

A flicker of hope came into the young man's blue eyes. 'Do you really think so?'

'I'm sure of it. Even if we get a substitute for you we can always do with another pair of hands.'

Ken sighed, and an involuntary twinge of pain marred his cheerful expression for a moment.

'I suppose Samantha is fast asleep.'

'Would you like to say good-bye to her? I'll go and get

her,' said Perry.

Wretched girl! She had not even come near Ken last evening, because she said she could not bear to think of his injury and she had been terrified at the sight of blood. She had not been so squeamish about the hunt, had she? But perhaps faced with the reality of Ken's accident, it had been too much for her.

'No, of course not, let her sleep,' said Fabian.

So she was forced to let Ken go off without seeing Samantha again. Trust Fabian to interfere, thought Perry. As they set off in the dark, Perry reflected that she would never have believed it a few weeks ago if anyone had told her she would trust herself to go out into the desert with an injured man and only Fabian to find the way.

'How will we get there?' she could not help asking. 'However do you know you're going in the right direction?'

Fabian laughed. 'I'm well equipped – I have a compass. But don't worry. Even though I have modern equipment, I can find my way by natural methods too. Like a yachtsman, I plot my way by the stars. Some people use the Southern Cross, but I favour Orion's Belt. The third star in the middle to the right always rises due east and sets due west of you, no matter where you may be. The Bushmen say that Orion is made up of tortoises hanging upon a stick. I suppose that's because Orion becomes visible at the time when the tortoises begin to become active at the beginning of spring.'

'Spring? I can't imagine that it's near spring here.'

'Oh, yes. It's the dry season now, but one day quite soon the rains will come, and then the miracle happens. Overnight leaves and flowers will burst from the bushes; lilies will grow in the waterholes; insects will come as if from nowhere and the birds will return.'

'Will we stay long enough to see it, do you think?'

'Who knows? It doesn't last long. In no time at all the young growth is scorched by the intense heat. Like youth or love, it's over soon.'

'You sound rather cynical,' she commented.

'Do I? I thought it was you who didn't believe in love, you who'd found that it goes too quickly.'

By the light of the dashboard, she could see his smile and felt he was mocking her.

'I didn't say that. I think some people do find a love that lasts. But young love is soon cut down, especially if other people interfere.'

'So you think young love is a delicate growth that can be scorched like the flowers in the desert? But I would have thought if love is real it could outlast other people's opposition.'

He had not experienced love as a young girl feels it, she thought. He was a hard man, not subject to gentle emotions. She did not reply, but sat silently as the truck lurched through the rough sand and bush. Occasionally Ken moaned, but Fabian had drugged him so extensively that he was not fully conscious. Far away near the horizon, Perry saw an orange glow.

'What's that?' she asked. 'It can't be the dawn, it's in the wrong place.'

'It's a grass fire,' said Fabian. 'This is the time of year when you get them in the desert. Everything is so tinder-dry that the sun flashing on a shiny pebble can start one. So long as they remain on the horizon and don't come any nearer we'll be all right.'

Perry thought she would be glad when the real dawn came, for with the light Fabian might make a bit smoother progress. They had padded the space around Ken with foam rubber cushions, but even so he moaned occasionally even though unconscious, and Perry was afraid that their bumping progress was doing him harm. When eventually it became light, she found little comfort in the scene before them, for the sun itself seemed like a living presence, an enormous weird face, rising red and distorted above the yellow haze of the fires that seemed to have spread now to several points upon the horizon. Everything looked so desolate in this part of the country. There were few trees and the yellow grass stretched in an endless lonely plain with black stunted bushes here and there. But at least it was flatter and made it easier to travel a bit more smoothly. Perry turned to look at Ken. He was very pale, his skin grey under the tan.

'Do you think he's lost a lot of blood?' she asked.

'I know he did, but he's strong, Perry, and we couldn't have left him there in this condition. He needs blood transfusions. This is the only way. But we must get him to the air-strip as quickly as possible. According to my calculations we should soon pick up a track that's used by cattle drovers, then we'll make more progress.'

As the sun rose higher, the heat became intense and when they saw a grove of small trees in the distance, Perry said, 'Fabian, there hasn't been any shade for ages. Don't you think it would be a good idea to stop near those trees and see if we can make Ken more comfortable?'

'I didn't want to stop. But perhaps you're right. How does he look?'

'Not too good.'

'Very well then, but we mustn't waste much time.'

It was heavenly, thought Perry, to get away from the grinding noise of the truck and to experience quiet if only for a little while. There was utter silence here except for the swishing sound of the grass in the wind.

What was it that the women had been singing? Something about the grass sighing for the rain to come and my heart telling me I am alone and waiting for my lover. But there was no time for such thoughts. Perry set herself to the task of making Ken more comfortable, bathing his face in the iced water that was still cool in the flask, and readjusting the pillows. His eyes were closed, but he took her hand and murmured, 'Samantha, is that you? How good of you to come with me.' She had not the heart to tell him that she was Perry and that Samantha had remained behind. He closed his eyes and seemed to drift off into a deeper sleep. What a pity, thought Perry, that they could not stay here and let him have his sleep out – but Fabian was determined to get on to the air-strip.

'Couldn't we stay here a little longer and let him rest?' she asked.

'Just long enough to get something to eat,' Fabian replied. 'We won't get another chance, and you hardly ate anything before we set out.'

The thought of food sickened Perry after the jolting journey in the truck. She turned away when Fabian pressed her to eat some rye biscuits topped with meat extract.

'Come on, Perry, no nonsense now. You must eat this. You'll need your strength for this journey.'

'It won't be much good if it makes me ill, will it?'

But his expression was unyielding and to her own surprise she took a bite of the food he had made her take in her hand. It was true she was hungry. The slight headache and feeling of nausea disappeared and she felt stronger as she finished the biscuit down to the last crumb and drank some lemon barley from the flask to which Fabian had added glucose.

'That's better, my dear. Trust me to know what's

good for you in these conditions.'

'Of course, Fabian. You always know best.'

Her voice was demure, her eyes downcast, but she stole a quick glance to find out what impression her statement had made. He was grinning.

'That was rather naughty of you. You must be feeling better.'

'Where there are trees one might expect water. I think I'll go to see if there's a spring. If there is, it would be wise to fill the flask from it just in case we need more water for bathing Ken's face. We have some, but you never know how much we may need.'

Fabian walked away and she saw his figure receding through the small grove. Ken was sleeping in the truck and she had packed everything in, but she felt reluctant to go back to her seat. She closed her eyes and gave herself up to enjoying the breath of wind that stirred the rustling dry leaves ever so slightly. How quiet it was! She wished they could stay here for a long time before they set out again on the wearisome journey. She was drowsy, almost asleep, when suddenly she was aware of running footsteps, dulled by the soft sandy ground. It was only because she was sitting with her head close to the ground that she heard the dull thud of them. At once her nerves were alert. She opened her eyes. Fabian was running towards her.

'Quick, get to the truck! There's a herd of buffalo not twenty yards away.'

She staggered up and as he came up to her he got hold of her by the waist and swung her up on to the seat.

'I doubt whether they saw me, but I wouldn't like to have to face a stampede. Buffaloes are such unpredictable creatures.'

He swung himself up beside her and suddenly there was a crackle of dry wood like tearing paper. The copse seemed to explode and half a dozen huge buffalo burst from out of the trees. They were so close that Perry was aware of the fusty warm cattle smell of their thick dusty pelts. When they saw the truck they halted for a moment, tossed their heavy heads, wheeled around and galloped off across the plain in another direction. Fabian let out a sigh of relief.

'Whew, that was close! Thank God they didn't choose to do that when we were sitting under the trees a little while ago. They usually run away when they see people, but if you confront them or if they think they're in danger, they can be perfect devils, more dangerous than any lion. They've got so much courage, they'll fight until they drop.'

He started the engine and they drove away.

'I suppose the moral is that we should inspect a grove of trees before sitting down. But there won't be much time for any more rest anyway.' He glanced down at Perry and squeezed her hand before quickly turning back to negotiating the track. 'Poor child, did you get a scare? Would you still have come on this trip if you'd known all the hazards you were going to face?'

'I think so,' said Perry, nettled by his term 'child'. 'Whatever happens I've had many thrilling experiences and I've seen things that I never expected to see, and just meeting the Bushmen has made the trip worthwhile.'

'I'm glad you think so. I do too. For me that's been the highlight of the expedition. I must say, Perry, you've proved to have more courage than I gave you credit for when we first met. However, the trip isn't over yet, not by a long way.'

Why must he always qualify any slight thing that sounded in the least complimentary? she thought, but he just was like that. By noon they reached the cattle track and were able to put on speed a little. The rest of the journey was uneventful, an endurance test full of heat and dust, and by late afternoon they came into the little settlement with its couple of trading stores and a one-storeyed hotel.

Ken woke up when the truck stopped and seemed much more aware of things than he had during the journey. Perry thought this was a good sign, and was even more relieved when they found that the pilot of the light aircraft was waiting to take him immediately to a hospital not very far away.

'I'll be fine. Don't worry about me,' Ken whispered to Perry as she bathed his face and tried to settle him more comfortably on the stretcher that the pilot had arranged in the plane. Fabian and Perry stood at the air-strip watching the small plane disappearing into the deep blue of the afternoon sky.

'Ken's a good chap. I'm sorry this had to happen,' said Fabian. 'However, I expect he may be able to come back. It depends how long it takes to get him better.'

They turned away and came back to the small white-washed hotel. It was strange to be in a building again. Although the rooms were clean, almost austere, with their shining green polished cement floors and grass mats and iron bedsteads with blue cotton counterpanes, after being used to the open air all the time, the atmosphere seemed close and heavy, smelling of the roast beef that was being prepared for dinner. Fabian left Perry sitting on the enclosed stoep with its arrangements of artificial flowers and its shabby wicker chairs and glass-topped tables, while he went to make arrangements about their rooms for the night. He came back carrying two glasses.

'This is one of the times when I approve of your taste for whisky. Drink that up before you go to your room to brush up for dinner. I would say you've earned it.

'Good news,' he added, as they sipped the reviving drink. 'A message has come that they're flying in a substitute for Ken. He's arriving by charter plane tomorrow morning, so we'll be able to start the journey back quite soon. I know this fellow. He's a good chap and has been working in wild life schemes for a number of years. He'll be an asset to our group.'

'I'm glad,' said Perry.

'I had thought that I might go to see some Bushman paintings that are not far from here. But we'll see how things pan out. In any case, if I go, I think you should remain here and have a rest before we start out on the journey back.'

She would have no choice even if she said she would like to see the paintings, she reflected, as she had the much-needed and refreshing bath before dinner; Fabian was so accustomed to command that he had not even asked her what she would like to do. She supposed he would take the other man with him if he went. Well, that would not matter. She felt as if she could sleep for twenty-four hours at least. But when she had bathed and put on the dark blue slacks and the glamorous Pucci print tunic with its flashing kingfisher colours she felt a new person. She had washed her red-gold hair and brushed it until it shone like burnished copper, then she applied make-up carefully and finished off with a coral lipstick, even applying turquoise eye-shadow that matched one of the colours in her tunic. I suppose it's silly to take such care in a small place like this, she thought, but somehow she had a desire to appear glamorous after all these days of living in khaki slacks and safari jackets.

'Perry, this is a change!' Fabian was waiting for her on the stoep and rose to take her arm and draw her towards the light. He smiled, eyeing her tunic. 'So you decided to pack that garment after all? Well, I must admit that tonight I can't consider it superfluous.'

The one or two people who were residents at the hotel had already dined and they found themselves alone in a small alcove away from the main dining-room. A softly shaded lamp shed down a golden pool of light, but beyond that there was shadow, and fluffy moths rustled in vain at the screened window. Perry thought they were both feeling a relaxation of tension after the strain of the journey and the anxiety about Ken. She had rather dreaded being alone with Fabian this evening, but he was in a light charming mood and very different from the man whose stern image she had carried with her since he influenced Mark to change his mind about marriage all those years ago. She was in such a happy mood herself now that this journey had passed without mishap that she forgot to be withdrawn and careful as she usually was with men. Fabian ordered a bottle of wine, and, although the meal was certainly not up to gourmet standards, the grilled fish, beef and Yorkshire pudding tasted delicious after the days in the desert. Fabian talked in an entertaining way about his travels and Perry found herself telling him about her life in Johannesburg and her work with Mike.

'It's odd,' he mused, when they were sitting on the deserted stoep with coffee and a liqueur that tasted of oranges, 'most girls, especially in South Africa, don't think their life is complete unless they've married. You're young still, of course, but you seem to have a cool attitude towards men and matrimony. Tell me, has something, some happening when you were a girl, put you against these things?'

She was tempted, very tempted, to tell him and to disclose the part he had played in the direction of her life, but even the wine had not made her as talkative as that. She yawned, and it was not really affected. She realized now how tired she was.

'Do you mind if I go to bed now? I'm exhausted.'

He had risen in a moment, apparently forgetting his question.

'Forgive me – I've been thoughtless keeping you talking. Go to bed and sleep well, my dear. You've been pretty wonderful today, Perry. I won't forget it.'

As she found her way across the open quadrangle behind the main buildings to the row of small whitewashed bedrooms, she could not disguise to herself the glow that she had felt when he said this. For once apparently he had appreciated something she had done, and all the discomfort and worry of this long day seemed worthwhile. A fan was whirring on the ceiling, stirring the warm air that seemed to her rather lifeless and stale after being used to sleeping in her little tent. She was glad she had brought the thin pale blue nightdress with its halter neck, for it was cooler to wear here and in the desert she had needed more practical pyjamas. She lay on top of the bed and tried to sleep, but the noise of the fan and the swish of the air as it followed its slow cumbersome route was disturbing. At last, however, she fell asleep.

She did not know how long her sleep had lasted when all at once she was aware of another noise, a fluttering that was surely not that of the fan, but surely too big for a moth. She lay for a while hoping the noise would go away, but it seemed to get louder. There was not even a glimmer of moonlight in the room and it was very dark. At last she felt she must get up to settle her mind as to the character of the intruder. It hardly sounded like a staghorn beetle, for they made a banging noise and this was more like the fluttering of a bird. Yes, that was what it must be. With that she plucked up her courage to turn on the bedside light.

A large bat was clinging to the iron rail at the bottom of her bed. Perry let out a scream of horror. If there was one thing she hated it was the thought of spending the rest of the night with a bat in the room. She had always had something that amounted almost to a phobia about the creatures. Before she could decide what to do next there was a light tap at the door.

'Perry, for God's sake, why did you scream? Are you dreaming, or is there something wrong?'

She flung open the door and hurled herself at Fabian.

'Take it away, take it away,' she implored. 'There's a huge bat in my room!'

Fabian laughed. His protective arms tightened around her.

'A bat? Thank heaven! I thought you'd found a snake in your bed.'

'But how can I get rid of it?'

She had recovered a little from her fright and tried to slip from his grasp, but he held her close, still smiling teasingly.

'We'll turn out the light and let it settle, then I can deal with it.'

Through the window that faced on to the courtyard they could see the bat flying with wild swoops backwards and forwards across the light.

'Come and sit on this seat while I turn off the light. We'd better choose a dark corner because the flying ants are out. That's what attracted the bat in the first place, I expect.'

Termite ants were fluttering around a lamp that had been left alight at the corner of the building, making a rustling sound as they took their nuptial flight with silver wings that they were to lose as soon as they dropped back to the ground.

'It's a sign that the rains can't be far off,' said Fabian. 'They tell me they had a small shower here yesterday. You may see spring in the desert after all.'

He drew her down to the seat and seemed in no hurry to go back to deal with the bat. Perry was aware all at once that she had come out of the room with no covering but the scanty halter-necked nightdress, and she shivered. His arm came around her, but firmly she shrugged it away.

'Fabian, please do something about that horrible creature!'

'Very well, but it seems a pity. It's much pleasanter sitting here.'

Alone at last, she sat watching the silver wings of the termites fluttering in gauzy transparency against the light. Fabian probably thought she had acted in a ridiculous fashion. His fleeting approval for her part in yesterday's journey would be cancelled by her cowardice about the bat. But she could not help the shudder of repulsion that was aroused at the thought of the weird creature in her room.

'It's gone,' Fabian said. 'It won't worry you again.'

She did not ask him what he had done to it – she preferred not to know. He had a hatred of killing wild creatures of whatever kind and she did not want to be blamed for another death. Perhaps he had just let it go. She hoped if he had done this it would not come back. But she did not ask him. He had brought her gown with him and slipped it over her shoulders.

'Stay a little,' he said, 'and calm down. You were a nervous wreck back there only on account of a poor little bat – and yet you face the hazards of the desert quite bravely.'

'It seems different somehow here.'

'Yes, did you find it stuffy sleeping with a roof over your head?' And as she nodded, 'It seems a pity to go in on a warm night. It's much pleasanter out here. Don't you agree?'

It was pleasant. The warm air was stirred occasionally by a cool breath of wind and the stars hung low. It could not be far from the dawn. But she did not want to be too near to this man with his protective arms that could tighten as if he felt some other kind of emotion.

'Let's stroll for a while,' she suggested.

'Stroll?' He grinned as if he saw through her device to get away from the seat where he was sitting so near to her in the darkness.

'Just along the village street,' she pleaded.

There was not even a sidewalk and the road was not smooth. It was odd to be walking where there were buildings. Not a soul was stirring. They seemed to be the only wakeful people in the little town. They had not walked very far when she stumbled on the uneven ground. He caught her arm and the next moment what she had been trying to prevent happened. She was in his arms. His head came down and he kissed her in a long hard embrace before she broke away from him. The stars seemed to be spinning overhead and she felt breathless and unsteady. Odd, in Johannesburg she always felt able to deal crisply and certainly with this kind of situation, but with this man she had a feeling of helplessness as if it were he who was in command. She pulled herself away from him, repressing the surprising emotion that had surged up when his firm hands encircled her as if he had placed a golden chain around her waist.

'We must go back,' she whispered, trembling.

He was a dark shadow beside her, holding her to him,

but he nodded his head and started to walk slowly back the way they had come. When they reached the door of her room he did not attempt to kiss her again as she had feared might happen. He looked down at her with grave grey eyes, for once not teasing or mocking her.

'Go to bed, Perry, and may there be no more bats or other creepy-crawlies tonight. Mark's plane will be in tomorrow morning. I'm hoping he'll get here quite early.'

'Mark?' Perry shivered, and this time it was not because of the cold dawn breeze that was already blowing away the stars.

'Mark Winthrop. He's becoming quite well-known in the wild life field. We're fortunate to get him. I always wanted him to come on this expedition, but he was tied up at the time. Now he's free. He's an excellent man. I've known him since he was a boy.'

'I too,' said Perry. It had slipped out, this thing that she had meant he should never know.

'You?' The light from the courtyard was shining on her face and he seemed to detect some expression that she had hoped was hidden. At the same time some kind of realization seemed to dawn on him. He frowned darkly.

'Why do you look like that?' cried Perry.

'He's the one – the man that you loved and from whom you were separated. I've thought all along there must have been something of the kind.'

'Yes,' Perry admitted. Oh, he was clever, this man. He could detect one's innermost feelings even if he had little sympathy for sentiment.

'But how was it that you were separated?' he asked. 'I would have said you would be very well suited to Mark as I know him. He's a fine man and very clever in his profession. He should go far. Who could have thought you weren't suitable for each other?'

Perry began to laugh. The varying emotions of the last hour had played upon her nerves as the young Bushman played the taut strings of his guachi.

'You did,' she said. 'You, Fabian. You separated us from each other. You advised Mark that he was not to marry me, that he was to put his career first. We parted and we've never seen each other since. Yes, you're the man whom I can thank for a life of empty years.'

CHAPTER NINE

NEXT morning when Perry was awakened by a knock on the door, she could not think for a moment where she was. The white-painted walls, the rough beams above her head, were so different from the green gloom of her little tent. Then she remembered.

'Come in,' she called sleepily.

A smiling African maid in a blue overall came in bearing a tray of coffee, placed it on the bedside table and silently withdrew. Perry lay there gradually awakening. The events of the night before seemed like a dream. Mark! Could it be true that he was really arriving here today? She raised herself on her elbow and poured the coffee. She had started to sip it when she noticed a slip of paper tucked under the sugar basin. Unfolding the note, she saw black clear handwriting sprawling across the page: 'Dear Perry, By the time you get this I will be on my way to see the Bushman paintings I mentioned yesterday. I've borrowed a smaller vehicle. It isn't far and I should be back in time for a late breakfast, so we can be on our way back to camp today. I thought after last night's conversation that you would welcome the chance to meet Mark alone. Good luck the second time around. Fabian.'

Oh, heavens, why had he done this? She did not know which would be worse, to meet Mark for the first time after all these years conscious of Fabian's mocking gaze, or to meet him alone and try to disguise the emotions she was bound to feel. But as she sipped her coffee she began to feel revived. Of course Fabian was right. It was maddening, but he usually was. It would be wonderful to meet Mark again on her own. He was not expecting to meet her, so she could observe his reaction, for he would not have had time to think about it. A feeling of thrilling dread intermingled with joy filled her whole being. She sprang up and looked in the small mirror of the cheap wooden dressing table. Eyes the colour of amber, in their fringe of dark gold-tipped lashes, stared back at her, distended and anxious. Gold-red hair gleamed in the sunshine that was already creeping in at the window. Had she changed very drastically? She tried to remember the innocent trusting face of the young girl Mark had known and to relate it to the experienced, sophisticated good looks of the career girl she had become. What would he think of her? She would soon know.

She showered and dressed carefully, regretfully discarding the more glamorous clothes she had worn last night in favour of blue denim jeans and a plain navy blouse. She brushed her hair until it shone and looked with some dissatisfaction at the golden tan that had covered her usually creamy skin. The owner of the hotel met her at the reception desk.

'Mr. Sinclair asked me to lend you a car to go to the air-strip. It's only an old Ford, but you'll find it easier to drive than the truck. You know the way, don't you? A message came to say that the plane should be in during the next fifteen minutes.'

She stood there trying not to think, concentrating on the windsock that was distended by the morning breeze, for if she thought that in a few minutes she was to meet Mark, something seemed to happen inside her, a quivering of nerves that she found difficult to control. At last it appeared, a small jet-engined plane, growing swiftly from a small gleam in the sky to a huge bird that filled the heavens with tearing noise. And then it was down and the shrieking engine was silenced. She watched as the plane door opened, unable to move so filled was she with tremulous joy and fear. The man who descended from the plane was shorter and stockier than the Mark who existed in her memory. There was some delay as he bade farewell to the pilot and the plane started to taxi slowly to the hangar. Then he looked around and seeing the car parked some way from the runway he picked up a suitcase and started walking towards it. She had thought when she saw him she would run towards him, but at the last moment she felt shy and confused, almost as if she were the young girl who had parted from him all those years ago.

Now he was only a few yards away and it was his turn to stand amazed. Then he put down his suitcase and quickened his step. His eyes were still that wonderful blue that had fascinated her as a girl, but his hair seemed darker, crisp and streaked with the sun. The clear skin of the young boy had been replaced by a brown weatherbeaten complexion with small crisscross lines around the eyes. But he was a good-looking man – possibly better-looking than she remembered. His smile was still the same as he stood before her and took her hand.

'Perry, am I dreaming? It can't be you, surely.'

She nodded, ashamed of the tears that came to her eyes. 'What are you doing here?'

She explained the situation as she led the way to the car. After that first handshake he had not attempted to touch her, and she was glad of this. He volunteered to drive, and she relinquished the wheel, glad of the opportunity as he examined the gears to wipe away the tears from her eyes without his noticing. For now that this dramatic meeting was over, she was conscious of a feeling of anticlimax. What had she expected? How ridiculous to expect that they would start again by feeling the same emotions they had felt for each other eight years ago. They had both grown older and they had been leading different lives. But somehow she felt let down. Her romantic dream of Mark did not coincide with the reality of the stocky, pleasant-looking man at her side. The terrific thrill that she had felt merely to be with him had gone. But she had scarcely spoken to him. She cast around in her mind for something to say.

'Did you have a good journey?' she asked.

'Very pleasant,' he said. 'We ran into a bit of storm, but it was soon over.'

His voice had changed. When she had known him before it had been the eager young voice of an enthusiastic boy, now it was the voice of a man, pleasant, courteous but indifferent. He turned to give her a swift glance as he negotiated the bumpy road to the little town.

'This is great to see you again. I never expected it, especially here. We'll have lots to talk about, but we'll save it for when we get to our destination. By the way, where is Fabian? I had expected he would meet me.'

'He's gone to see some Bushman paintings. It isn't too far away. He said he would be back for a late breakfast.'

'Trust Fabian to make the most of being here. I should have thought he would have had enough of travelling yesterday. It must have been pretty rough bringing an injured man in. Not the kind of thing I would have imagined you doing, Perry.'

How did he know, she thought, what kind of thing she would do? He did not know her now.

'I wouldn't have thought photographing the desert was quite your line of country,' he said when she had explained her role in the expedition. 'You must be a little more rugged than I remember. I've heard occasionally of your work in Johannesburg. Once I saw some of your photographs at an exhibition. They were very good, very sophisticated, indoor stuff, models and so on.'

So he had thought about her sufficiently to take an interest in her work. Perry was touched. Perhaps after all they would find some common ground. But at the moment she felt she was talking to a stranger. And she felt this even more so as they sat over breakfast. He had said they would find plenty to tell each other, but the inspiration they had always found in each other's company had vanished. Before her was a pleasant enough man, a little taciturn when it came to conversation so that she found herself struggling not to have large gaps of silence. He was different in this respect from Fabian, she thought. However annoying, conversation with Fabian was easy; they always had something to say to each other.

She began to feel depressed. Was it not possible to experience the emotions again that she had felt when she was a girl? Had love vanished for ever? She had never felt interest in any other man because she had always thought that her feelings could not equal the love she had felt for Mark, and yet here he was sitting at the breakfast table with her and she was wondering what to say to him next. She found herself wishing that Fabian would return. He had said he would not be long and he had been away for some hours having started off in the early part of the morning.

'How far away are these paintings?' she asked the hotel keeper, unable to conceal her restlessness and eagerness to start back to the encampment.

'Only a few miles away and very easy to find. Mr. Sinclair must have found them more interesting than likely because I would have thought he would have been back long ago. He said he wanted to start back at eight.'

It was after nine. If they were to accomplish the journey by daylight, they should be on their way. What could be keeping Fabian?

'Let's pack the truck and be ready,' said Mark, obviously as eager as she was to get going. 'If he isn't back in another half hour we'll go in search of him. The route there is quite clearly defined, I understand.'

'There's a trapdoor on to the roof. Perhaps you would like to take the glasses and look over the desert from there. You should be able to see the jeep coming back,' the manager suggested.

They went up a ladder on to the roof. In the distance lay the desert, mile upon mile. Mark was the first to look through the glasses.

'Good God!' he exclaimed. Perry felt a twist of fear. 'There are bush fires in several places near the track. I think Fabian may have run into difficulties. I'll take the truck and go after him, perhaps I can collect some Africans to help.'

'Let me come too,' Perry demanded.

'I hardly think you need to do that. It would be best if you waited here.'

'But I understand the truck. I could drive it if necessary.'

Perry had seized on the first excuse she could think of. She felt determined to go in search of Fabian. She found she could not stand the idea of being left here alone to wait and wonder what was happening.

'All right,' said Mark.

He seemed as if he could not bother to argue with her because he was in such a hurry to get going. He spoke to the manager, who produced a quantity of sacks which they soaked with water, and he himself joined them with a number of the servants from the hotel. He brought some wet towels too, explaining that if they had to go through smoke it would be best to have these available. As they reached the outskirts of the town and came into the open desert, they could see the grey pall of smoke from the fires that were all around and stretching to the horizon.

'It's the time for fires in this part of the world,' said the hotel manager. 'The driest time of year. Soon the rains will come and we'll be safe for a while longer.'

They bounced along the rugged track and all the time Perry was hoping desperately that she would see the jeep that Fabian had borrowed coming along in the opposite direction. Why was she so frightened? Fabian was experienced in desert life. He could look after himself. There was no need to feel this desperate confusion, this secret heavy dread that seemed to clutch at her very heart. And now they came to a place where there was an outcrop of rocks towering up rather surprisingly above the neighbouring scrub.

'There's the jeep,' exclaimed Mark. 'So where's Fabian?'

As he spoke there was a crackling noise to the right and a burning wall of fire appeared shimmering near to the rocks.

'He must have been cut off by the fire. He probably found the paintings but now can't get back to the jeep.'

'I hope you're right,' said the manager, 'and that he's safe behind that wall of fire. It looks pretty dangerous to me.'

But nevertheless he went towards it giving quick instructions to the Africans who were evidently used to grass fires, for they started beating at the flames with wet sacks. Perry started to go towards the fire, but Mark shouted to her to get back and sit in the truck. She sat there feeling helpless as she watched them fighting the flames. They seemed to be getting on top of them, but where was Fabian? Suppose she were to take the truck and try to drive around the fire? It seemed to have died down at that end. Afterwards he could not think what had possessed her, but she put a wet towel around her mouth to keep out the fumes and started up the truck while the men were engaged with their fire-fighting and drove to where she could see the fire had swept past and there was nothing but a blackened patch. The only thought in her mind was that she must find Fabian. She could feel the heat of the flames, but they were roaring away from her. And now she was on the other side of the rocks. She stopped the truck and got out, searching with her eyes for some sign of movement above, where the stones formed a natural overhang like a cave. But she was suddenly startled by a voice close at hand.

'Perry – good God, what are you doing here? How did you get through the fire?'

She felt weak with relief. 'I drove it through the gap, Fabian, while the others were putting the fire out.'

'What a crazy thing to do! Why on earth did you do it?'

'I thought perhaps you needed help, that you'd been overcome by smoke.'

Fabian grinned. 'Not me. Didn't you know I lead a charmed life? But you . . . you could have easily lost the truck for us – and how are the tyres?'

She had not thought about them. She had not thought of anything but that Fabian was in danger behind that wall of flame. And now she found that instead of being considered somewhat heroic she appeared to have done something foolish.

'They seem to be all right. That part of the ground

must have been cooled by the wind. But it would have been better if you'd left me to make my way back on my own. The boys seem to be coping quite adequately with the fire, but really there was no cause for alarm. It was merely annoying that I was delayed. If you'd waited, the fire would have swept past. I was never in any danger.'

How aggravating he was, standing there with his maddening confidence, his grey eyes alight with teasing laughter. Why had she been so concerned about him? Certainly he did not deserve a moment's worry from her. The fire had died down now and he took the driver's seat in the truck and motioned to her to climb up beside him. Something in her expression must have struck him, for he put his arm around her and held her close.

'What is it, Perry? Why do you look upset?'

She tried to blink away the tears, but to her immense chagrin they spilled over on to her cheeks.

'Surely not tears? I wouldn't have thought it of you, Perry. I thought you were tough. Has the meeting with Mark been too much for you? How did it go, by the way?'

She made an enormous effort at self-control.

'The smoke got into my eyes. Mark? Oh, it was grand seeing him again after all these years.'

He might not have believed her explanation about the tears, but he made no further comment. His meeting with Mark saved any further conversation between them. But as they started back, on the long journey to the encampment and she sat between the two men, she was silent. They did not seem to notice this because Fabian was telling Mark about the progress of the expedition, but Perry was quiet because she was trying to make some kind of sense of the varying emotions she had felt today. The memory of Mark had been expunged from her mind by her meeting with the living man who was pleasant, certainly, but could never again arouse passionate love, she knew.

One man had aroused great emotion in her today. She was quiet because she was trying to face the fact and it filled her with a haunting despair. For it was madness that Fabian of all people should have made her feel that if anything were to happen to him, then life for her would not be worth living any more.

The small green tent seemed like a refuge and Perry would have dearly loved to plead tiredness and not have to face the evening ahead, but Samantha had insisted that they were to have a special celebration for Mark's arrival.

She had not even inquired after Ken. It seemed as if it was a case of out of sight out of mind with her. Instead she welcomed Mark with great enthusiasm. 'It's lovely to have someone new to look at and talk to,' she told him childishly. She had so much charm, thought Perry, that it did not seem to matter that she always said the first thing that came into her head. She was easily bored and it really was a wonder that Paul had prevailed upon her to stay as long. But of course Fabian was the attraction. Samantha found it a challenge to meet a man who did not immediately become attracted to her. And he was older than the type of man she was used to. But Mark was more attractive than Ken, thought Perry. Poor Ken! He had seemed so devoted to Samantha, and really he had not seemed to stand a chance.

Paul had amused himself by doing some shooting and was proud of the fact that they were to have a brace of guinea-fowl for their evening meal. It was a moonlit night and the warm wind brought to the camp the smell of grass. As soon as she saw the glowing light of the fire Perry began to feel a little more cheerful. It was good to be back. She must put aside the question of her feelings for Fabian. That was absolute nonsense, brought about by the set of circumstances, the meeting with Mark, the adventure of the grass fire. Now she would make herself busy with practical things. What a darling little Topaz was! The prints of his paws around her tent were like little flowers. He had an immense curiosity about everything that moved, and pounced upon leaves blowing in the wind. He licked Perry with his rasping tongue and purred when she petted him as if he was pleased that she had returned.

The guinea-fowl tasted very good that evening. Samantha was wearing her dark long cotton dress and looked enchantingly feminine bending over her guitar and plucking a nostalgic tune from its strings. Fabian produced a bottle of champagne which he had cooled in the small freezer.

'What's the celebration?' asked Paul. 'Apart from the fact, of course, that I had good hunting while you were away.'

'We're celebrating a reunion,' Fabian replied. 'Our meeting with Mark.'

Perry was glad he had not expanded on this. Was he trying to make up for the injury he had unwittingly inflicted upon her all those years ago? Was he encouraging her to make up for the long separation with Mark? Was that why he referred to a reunion? But it was too late for that, she realized now. She was glad she had met Mark again. It had given her a new perspective. The champagne slid down her throat, its cold bubbles seeming an alien taste in these austere surroundings. Samantha seemed to be engaging Mark's attention and Paul came and sat by Perry's side.

'You're looking lovely tonight, Perry, in spite of that tiresome journey. You have a kind of radiance like a woman in love.'

'Thank you, Paul, but you pay the most odd compliments. Who could I be in love with?'

'Who indeed?' His shrewd green eyes glanced speculatively from Fabian to Mark. 'Well, if I had a pretty woman to myself at a hotel on the edge of the desert, I might be tempted to make the most of it. Be careful, my dear. Fabian, although he seems a little cold, has a reputation with women. My daughter, young as she is, could cope with a man like him better than you could, Perry.'

'You're quite wrong, Paul. I don't know how this conversation started anyway.'

'It started because you have a secret kind of glow about you tonight.'

They were interrupted by Fabian, who had raised his glass. 'To old friends reunited,' he said.

'Who are we drinking to?' asked Samantha. 'You and Mark, Fabian?'

'And Perry,' Fabian informed her. 'She and Mark are old friends.'

'So that's it! Now I understand,' whispered Paul. 'Forgive me, Perry. I had the wrong idea altogether. I thought Fabian had been charming you on the desert journey.'

Perry felt confused. 'I wish you'd leave it alone, Paul.'

'I apologize, my dear. I'm glad for my daughter's sake that it isn't Fabian.'

He's ridiculous, thought Perry. She was lying on a long cushioned seat that was one of the luxuries Fabian had provided for his guests. Paul had insisted on her using it while he had the humbler camp stool. From the chair she could gaze up into the dark blue vault of the heavens where the pale moon was chasing the stars. If she glanced to her left she could see Fabian, his face glowing in the lamplight, talking to Samantha and Mark with his easy charm. Why did she feel herself suddenly so drawn to him? Why did she wish she was alone with him again, alone in the shadowy moonlit street of the little desert outpost? This was madness, a crazy desire inspired by the dazzling bubbles of the golden drink she held in her hand.

She was glad of the distraction when Samgau walked from the direction of the Bushman camp with Toma and Natamu. He told them that the Bushmen were going to celebrate the fact that they had had the feast of gemsbok meat by dancing and playing games. Would they like to see this? Fabian was indestructible, thought Perry, for in spite of the fact that they had travelled for two days he sprang to his feet with great enthusiasm.

'What about it, Perry?' he called across to her. 'Do you feel up to taking any photographs? Is your flash loaded?'

Wood had been heaped upon the fires in the Bushman village and the savoury smell of roasted meat was in the air. Smoke lay around the encampment in a blue haze and a big circle had been left empty near the fire where the girls were sitting in a group clapping their hands and singing. But the men were still grouped around the small fires near the huts, smoking and talking to each other. The children took the opportunity to play in the cleared space. The little girls were imitating springboks, prancing around and pretending to pluck at tufts of grass. The little ones were the baby animals and the boys stalked them pretending to be lions. Every now and again there would be a cry of alarm and the girls would group around the younger children while the boys as lions attacked sometimes to carry them off. Then they did a frog dance, imitating frogs with lifelike jumps as children do all over the world.

Nusi came up to Perry as she was trying to photograph the children. She was looking lovely tonight, though her expression was still sad. Her skin was the colour of honey, her tufted hair hanging with shining white beads and her leather apron skirt adorned in intricate patterns. She smiled shyly and handed Perry an object wrapped in grass.

'What is this?' asked Perry, and Nusi shook her head shyly, pointing her hand to Perry with a lovely gesture of the long delicate fingers. Fabian had come up to them, for he was anxious to give Perry advice about the photography.

'Open it up. Nusi wants you to look at her gift.'

It was a bow and arrow in miniature, exquisitely made. 'Oh, how lovely!' exclaimed Perry. 'Imagine Nusi making such a tiny thing, and it's so perfect.'

'You're favoured,' said Fabian. 'Do you know its significance?' And when she shook her head, 'It's the love bow and it's used to give the owner good fortune either in love or in hunting. Nusi evidently wishes that you should be lucky in love as she herself wants to be.'

'Poor Nusi,' said Perry. 'I'm afraid my scheme didn't bring her much luck.'

Fabian smiled, but there was something hard about the expression of his eyes. 'Your magic bow has come at the right time for you, the night we're celebrating your reunion with Mark.'

She wanted to deny this, to fling aside his cool assumption that now she had met Mark again she would fall into his arms and live happily ever after. She did not feel this was the case at all. But with this man she felt as if she were hammering against a wall of stone. He drew his own conclusions and nothing would alter them. The children had withdrawn from the arena of sand and the singing of the women grew louder, sweet and piercing so that it set Perry's nerves throbbing. It was filled with sadness and desire for something that could not be. Love and pain were mingled, happiness and grief. It was the song she had heard before, but this time it continued on and on with longing and loneliness and passion.

'What does it mean?' she asked Fabian. He had drawn her away from the circle and motioned to her to sit down on the grass. He sat very close beside her, his eyes on the women, so that he could tell her when he thought the moment to photograph them had come.

'What? Oh, yes, the song . . . Samgau told me what it means, more or less . . . I cry by the fire alone, because the earth is dry under the sun. It is crying all day long for the rain to come and I am like the earth, I too weep because I wish that my lover would come and carry me away. The grass cries for the wind to get the rain to come and my heart cries too because I am alone.'

There was all the longing and loneliness in the world in the voices of these small primitive women, and then suddenly the note changed. From the darkness beyond the firelight, the men came dancing swiftly into the place in front of the women, and they too were singing. Fabian had taken Perry's hand and drawn her to her feet and for a moment she swayed against him.

'Be ready to photograph this,' he said.

'What is it they're singing now?' she asked.

There must be a reply, she felt. That wild longing in the women's voices must be appeased in some way.

'They say something like this . . . Listen to the wind, you will hear the rain coming. Listen to your heart, for you will hear that your lover is coming.'

'So they get their answer. It comes right in the end,' she said.

'Yes, Perry, it comes right in the end, as I hope it will come right for you and Mark. Now let's go to photograph the dancing.'

But it could not come right, she thought dully as she got on with her task. For Mark was not the answer to her dreams. As the men danced, there was a hard rattling noise from the cocoons filled with fragments of ostrich egg that were tied to their ankles. The clapping and singing of the women and the stamping of the men's feet together with the hard noise of the rattles all harmonized in a peculiar rythmical way that had no need of other musical instruments. It seemed as if it was likely to go on and on. When Perry had taken adequate photographs, she asked Fabian if he would mind if she went back to the camp. She felt exhausted both physically and mentally.

'Very well, if you must,' he said a little shortly. 'Leave the camera with me in case I get an opportunity to take one of them falling into a trance. I believe that can happen when they've danced for a long time.'

She laughed, disguising her hurt at his abruptness. 'If I stay any longer, Fabian, you'll be able to see me falling into a trance, I'm quite sure. I'll just slip away.'

'No, you mustn't go by yourself. Take Mark with you. That's what you'd like, isn't it?'

Before she could deny this he had called to Mark who was deep in conversation with Samantha.

'I'm talking to Mark,' Samantha pouted. 'Surely Perry can find her way back on her own.'

'Of course I can,' said Perry, now thoroughly distressed by Fabian's insistence that she should have Mark for an escort.

'No, you can't. I'm responsible for your welfare and

you must have some protection on the way back.'

'Oh, for heaven's sake, Fabian,' Samantha mocked. 'Perry's a big girl now, aren't you, Perry?'

Fabian was not to be persuaded.

'Mark can take Perry back and return if he wants to. It will only take a few minutes.'

Why was he pushing Mark at her? thought Perry. He could not realize that all feeling she had had for Mark was past. They walked away from the firelight. Mark had a torch and the path was quite clear, well trodden by all the Bushmen visitors to the camp.

'I'm sorry to drag you away, Mark, I could have easily come by myself. I don't know why Fabian was so fussy about it.'

'Think nothing of it. I'm pretty tired myself after the rush to come here and all the drama of the fire today.'

The walked the path in silence broken only by the sounds of the desert night; a screech owl flew overhead, its soft wings in silent flight, and a night plover sounded lonely as if it were calling to its mate.

'It's good to be here,' said Mark. 'It isn't strange to me, of course. I've visited the desert before – that's why Fabian got in touch with me. I tried to make a study of Bushmen some years ago. How do you like them, Perry?'

'I think they're amazing. They live in such rugged harsh conditions and yet they really are such a gentle kind of people, and so full of humour.'

'That's right. It isn't in their nature to fight. They have to use their wits, though, simply to keep alive.'

They had reached the camp by now and she was glad to see her lamp illuminating the small green tent, making it look like a giant glow-worm. Joshua had built up the fire and it was a cheerful sight after the darkness of the journey back from the Bushman village.

'We can't waste such a marvellous fire. What do you say, Perry? Come and sit a while; you haven't told me anything about yourself.'

She let herself be persuaded to sit down by the fire with Mark. She felt in a trancelike state as she had said, for she was exhausted, and yet she knew she would have difficulty in sleeping even if she went off to her tent. She had not yet had time to examine the significance of her feelings towards Fabian. Surely it could not be true? It had been brought on by the romantic circumstances of desert life, and the journey to the little town. She did not want to feel like this, to have the same sad, hopeless longing that she had sensed in the voices of the women as they sang. But that had come to a conclusion and this feeling of hers could not have any satisfactory ending. Fabian hardly noticed her and on the occasions when he had kissed her it was definitely only because he had this reputation for attracting women and found her attitude of coldness somewhat intriguing. She wished she could get away somewhere on her own, where she need not meet him for a while and could sort out her feelings and persuade herself to be the cool, sensible grown woman that she was in her Johannesburg life.

'You're very pensive.'

She had forgotten about Mark, sitting quietly beside her near the glowing fire.

'I'm sorry, Mark. You must think me rude. Tell me about yourself. You seem to have made a success of the career you chose.'

'Yes, Perry, I don't know what one would mean by success. I certainly haven't achieved fame. I'll never be as calculated in this field as Fabian, for instance. But it's been a good life, an interesting one. I wouldn't have had it any other way.'

'Wouldn't you?' she said.

He did not seem to realize that he had said something that could be hurtful. Had he forgotten how they had felt about each other all those years ago? Men got on with their lives, Perry thought. They did not brood over the past as much as women did.

'I suppose you must be married with a family?' she asked.

'No, no, Perry, I've never married. I became absorbed in my career and whenever I met a woman who attracted me I found myself thinking "Would she like to live in these wild far-away places that I have to live in?" and the answer always seemed to be no.'

As it was eight years ago, she reflected. Fabian's influence had lasted a long time.

'And you, Perry? You too have never married?'

'No. When you get older and have an interesting life of your own, somehow you seem to get choosey about men.'

He laughed. His eyes flashed blue in the firelight. He was a good-looking man and had grown better-looking with the years. She had not been wrong about that, but now he was like a handsome stranger.

'So we were right when we parted, Perry, isn't that so? If you'd married me, you wouldn't have had this exciting photographic career or your glamorous life in Johannesburg.'

'No, that's true, Mark.'

He turned towards her and held her arms lightly, turning her so that he could look full into her face.

'You've grown even lovelier than I remember,' he said softly. 'I'm glad we've had this chance to meet again. It will be good to know you once more, Perry, whatever comes of it.'

He leaned forward and kissed her softly, a kiss of friendship rather than passion. She wished, oh, how she wished that she could feel again the emotions that had touched her as a girl, but now she felt nothing but a warm affection of this pleasant man who was sitting by her side in the firelight.

'Sorry to interrupt,' came the voice of Fabian from the shadows. 'I've come for more film, Perry, the other is all used up.'

She sprang to her feet and went to find what he needed.

'You soon got over your tiredness,' he said rather sharply, when he had followed her to the truck that she used as a dark room. How could she explain that Mark had persuaded her to sit there for a while even though she was dropping with weariness? Fabian would think she was trying to shirk the photography.

'Would you like me to come back?' she asked. 'Are you going to take a lot more shots?'

'It depends very much on what happens. Natamu fell into a trance. He suddenly fell to the ground and seemed unconscious. Then he rose and touched us all, apparently to draw the evil from us. But certainly you mustn't come. I don't want to interfere again. You seem to be getting on very well with Mark, and, believe it or not, I would like to see him settled and married to someone who could make him happy. He's not really a loner like me. He would be happier with a wife and family.'

Almost as much as she had hated him once long ago for interfering with her life and parting her from Mark, she hated him now for pushing her the other way, and for encouraging her to make her life with Mark again. A loner – yes, that was what he was. However much women attracted him, he would never let them be anything else but an amusing pastime in his life. She was glad the bewildered feelings she had experienced since yesterday had changed now to this black dislike. Oh, how she wished she could get away from everyone!

CHAPTER TEN

IN spite of her fears to the contrary she slept soundly in her small green tent and still felt very sleepy when she was awakened at first light by a scratching noise against the canvas. Could it be Topaz? She peered out. No, he was still sound asleep in his box. What was it, then? She was startled by a sibilant soft whistle, and then in the half-light a small figure appeared before her.

'Nusi, what are you doing here?'

The girl put her hand to her lips and glanced quickly around, but nothing stirred. She indicated to Perry that she wanted a pad and pencil. In the days that had passed since she had made friends with Nusi, they had evolved a simple method of communication by drawing pictures that aided the gestures they made to each other. But now Perry thought that she must be mistaken in spite of the fact that she had always before managed to follow Nusi's meaning quite quickly, for it seemed to her that Nusi meant that she, Toma and small Kigi should go on a hunt today. Nusi had drawn a picture of little matchstick people following an antelope with bows and arrows, but one was obviously Perry, in a sun-helmet and slacks and shirt. She pointed to herself and said, 'You mean me?' . . . and when Nusi nodded, 'But what about the others?' gesturing to the other tents. Nusi shook her head. She wanted Perry, her friend, to come alone. She indicated that they would not walk far.

Toma had felt that some kind of game was somewhere not far away. Fabian had told Perry of this peculiar instinct that the Bushmen had to feel the presence of an animal almost in their bones. So this could be so. But what was she to do? Her whole desire was to consent. She had failed to get satisfactory pictures of the previous hunt and this would be a very good opportunity, because if she were on her own just with the three, Toma, Nusi and Kigi, she would have some hours away from the others, some time to herself beneath the dome of the blue desert sky, when she could be rid of all her bewildering thoughts during a day in this world beyond the camp, this place of immense restfulness and peace. She nodded to Nusi. 'Very well, I will come.'

She decided she would leave a message with Joshua, the cook, who was already stirring in the kitchen tent, and she armed herself with a few rye biscuits and a flask of lemon barley, for she hated to think what would be Toma and Nusi's fare that day. What a determined creature Nusi was! She had made up her mind that she was going to marry Toma and therefore he must kill an animal to prove his manhood. She had not accepted the fact that things had gone wrong with the first hunt, but here she was all ready to try again. Perry felt sure that it was against custom for an unmarried man and woman to go off on their own like this, and that was evidently why they were taking herself and little Kigi, for it was because of her friendliness that she was being taken, she thought. They had no real interest in her photography.

The little Bushmen were lithe and swift in spite of Toma's slight handicap. She realized she would have some difficulty in keeping up with them. It was scarcely yet light and the sun had not risen but was present as a stroke of apricot-coloured paint upon the great grey palette of the desert sky. They went quickly away from the encampment where as yet only Joshua was awake. In their tiny scherms, the Bushmen were all sleeping in the hollows of sand that were lined with grass like the nests of small birds. The grey light made the country look vast and lonely, but a warm wind was blowing and presently Perry heard the noise of bush doves singing. It was a soothing sound and again she was glad she had come on this expedition far away from the atmosphere of the camp that seemed to be for ever tense with the different play of personalities. She resolved that she would try to put all her thoughts about Fabian behind, to concentrate on the steady progress of the hunt, and presently she would try to take photographs that would make up for her previous failure.

Some small duiker scattered in alarm from amongst the bushes and Kigi chased after them, but soon gave up, for Toma and Nusi were after bigger game. The sun was rising now, splashing the heavens with streaks of flame. It was going to be hot, but then of course, it always was. Perry had, she thought, learned to ignore the intense heat of the desert and her sun-helmet would be adequate protection. It reached to the edge of her shirt collar and unlike the Bushmen no part of her was exposed.

Presently Toma motioned to them to pause. Amongst the small shrubs and grass in the patches of earth he had evidently found traces of the game he sought. There were marks of several hoofs, small footprints of antelope, clear cut in the hard ground. The grass around the tracks seemed newly trampled, their bruised moisture fresh and not dried out at all. Toma began to prepare his bow that had been carried slung over his shoulder together with his leather bag. He observed every sign of the trail with great concentration and Perry was glad of the pause, for it enabled her to get her camera ready and take some shots of Toma and of the marks on the ground. Then they went quietly ahead, coming out into more open country but still following the trail of the group of animals.

Suddenly over a ridge of sand they came upon a deep dry pan, an almost circular basin, golden yellow in the morning light, and upon the smooth floor of the pan was a little group of springbok. The animals paused for a moment, startled and curious, taking tentative steps towards the intruders, and then at a sudden movement of panic from one of them they were off, running up the further slopes making fantastic leaps, hoofs bunched together, bodies arched, flaunting the silky gossamer hair that spread like small fans upon their backs. They bounced up and down as if, thought Perry, they were on a trampoline. They were so beautiful that she experienced a bitter regret that Toma was about to attempt to shoot one of them. Their chocolate and white pelts gleamed splendidly in the ray of the sun, and with their fantastic leaps they seemed magical as if they were half animal, half bird.

She had been very busy using her ciné and turned now away from the sight of the springboks to see what Toma was doing. To her surprise he had replaced his arrow and, making a hissing noise between his teeth as if to draw her attention, he pointed to a group of bushes on the outer side of the pan between themselves and the springbok. He said one word and it was a Bushman word she had learned from the children's visits to little Topaz. In the heat of the day a cold chill ran down her spine, for she knew the word meant 'Lion'. Three tawny shapes were slinking from the shadows of the bushes towards the fleeing springbok. The male, a big black-maned beast, paused, huge and terrifying, and watched while a lioness skilfully cut between one of the last springboks and drove it panic-stricken towards the other female. One leap from the lioness and the startled springbok was on the ground, its struggles hardly begun before a bite at the throat from the powerful jaws finished its life. The other springboks had vanished as if they had never existed and the lioness started to drag the carcase towards the bushes where her lord and master lay in the shade watching approvingly the results of her efforts.

'I must go back,' thought Perry, as panic-stricken as the poor springbok had seemed a few moments ago. 'Surely Toma and Nusi won't want to continue?'

But it seemed that they did. Evidently they considered that as the lions had made their kill they were no longer a danger to them. Toma motioned them to come around and work their way through the bush in the direction that the springboks had taken on the other side of the pan away from where the lions were tearing at their prey with bloodcurdling growls. Over the ridge of sand, Toma's pace quickened, for by the trail of the springboks he could tell that they were still running in panic. If he was to keep up with them, they would all have to go more quickly. It was getting hotter now. The sun had risen higher in the sky and seemed like a living presence, shouting, 'Look at me! Here I am. Nothing is more important than the heat I give.' The only reality to Perry was the catch of her heaving breath and the heat of the sun on her shoulders and the regular pounding sound of their footsteps upon the sunbaked ground.

On and on they went, following the trail of the springbok. The animals were slowing down now. Ahead of them Perry saw an outcrop of rocks to which the animals seemed to be heading for shelter. Toma smiled as if he thought he could succeed if they retreated to a place like this. There was a narrow defile through the rocks that must be a path used by game and Toma plunged into this closely followed by the others. How welcome the shade of the rocks was to Perry! Up on a ledge a hyrax gave its warning call followed by the harsh bark of a baboon. And suddenly on the ridge, quite close to them, there were the springbok. Nusi crept forward; acting like the lioness, she swarmed up the other side, cutting off the straggler from the main group and driving it towards Toma. He was there ready with his bow and let fly, catching the animal on the flank.

The springbok hesitated, then plunged after its companions. Perry gave an exclamation. Had he failed again? But Toma did not think so. He replaced his quiver before making ready to follow the little group of fleeing animals. He was sure now of his success, smiling at Nusi and laughing as Kigi turned head over heels, somersaulting to express his excitement. Perry was just as excited, for she had got some good shots of the hunt and her sorrow at the killing of the springbok was overcome by her joy that now Toma and Nusi should get their desire. They all felt a renewal of energy as Toma pursued the animal that was swiftly dying from the effect of the poisoned arrow. There was not long to wait. Soon it sank to its knees and Toma went towards it to give it a merciful release from any suffering. There was a kind of reverence in the way he did this. Perry had noticed before how much at one the Bushman seemed to be with the animal that he had put to death.

She had taken all the shots she intended to do for the time being and now she left the scene of the killing, glad to get away for a while, and climbed a little way to where she could see a rock overhang which would provide shade. It formed a natural cave but open to the light and on the smooth surface of the rocks she was startled to see there were pictures. Why, these must be Bushman paintings, the kind Fabian had gone to see when the fire occurred. As she peered at them, they became more clear, small drawings of stick-like people but with an amazing sense of real motion, tawny paintings of antelopes and other animals. She remembered now that

Fabian had said they were done by Bushmen some hundreds of years ago, but the art seemed to have become lost to succeeding generations. Fabian would be thrilled if he could come here, and she looked forward eagerly to being able to tell him about them. As she tilted her head to look at the paintings higher on the rocks, her sun-helmet was dislodged from her head and rolled down on to the rocks below. No matter. She could easily get it later, for she knew Kigi would climb down on to the rocks like a little goat and could easily retrieve it. She was in the shade now, so she would not miss it.

It was good to be without the hat anyway. She felt a coolish breeze blowing between the rocks and lifting the damp tendrils of red-gold hair upon her forehead. This was the first opportunity she had had to rest, and now thoughts came rushing back to her about the events of the past few days. She wished with all her heart that she had not told Fabian about her previous connection with Mark and the part he himself had played in separating them. For now, strange as it might seem, he appeared to want to bring them together again. And it was too late. Mark no longer attracted her. She found herself wishing ruefully that he did, for she did not want to examine the other feelings that seemed to come so close to the surface of her mind, however hard she tried to conceal them. She did not like Fabian. He was impatient, often harsh and seemed to have no comprehension of any tender feelings. But I love him, she thought, horrified by her own admission. I don't care what he's like. It doesn't matter at all. He's Fabian. I love the way he laughs when he's amused. I love the way his grey eyes can look like the flash of steel when he's annoyed. I know I should try to get over this, and I will, for he has no feeling for me. When I get back to Johannesburg, I'll get over it, she promised herself. I'll go back to my own life. But when she thought of this life, it seemed to her that nothing was as important as the time she had spent here in this land of endless yellow plains where one lived so close to nature and where the Bushmen in spite of their harsh lives seemed to have found the gift of happiness.

She was so deep in thought that she had not been conscious of her surroundings, and now she was startled by the harsh 'bom-bom' of a baboon quite close to her. He was perched upon some rocks a few yards away and he had not noticed her because he was watching some younger baboons playing down below. To her dismay she realized that one of them had seized her sun-helmet and was examining it with great curiosity. Another bigger one approached him and tried to tear the interesting object away, but the first one held on to it, uttering indignant grunts. She saw that under their combined assault the hat was taking a severe battering. She wanted to shout, but was scared of the reaction of the big guard baboon who was near her. With sinking heart she saw them seize the remnants of her hat and toss it amongst the rocks.

Just then Nusi and Kigi appeared below, but they were too late. The baboons seized the remains of the hat and ran up the rocks clambering swiftly with their queer loping gait. Kigi was in fits of laughter, giving a good imitation of the animals, and Toma and Nusi were laughing too. Perry wondered what she should do. She thought with dread about the long stretch of desert country that she would have to traverse hatless before getting back to the camp. The Bushmen, of course, hardly seemed to feel that heat and did not need any head covering, so they could scarcely be expected to realize the seriousness of her position. She hoped they would wait a while until the great heat of the day had passed, but they were evidently eager to get back with their prize. She had a scarf at her throat and now she knotted it to place on her head. It was thin, but better than nothing.

Toma had slung the dead springbok around his neck and the weight he had to carry made the journey back much more slow. They were all tired, but Perry roused herself to take more shots of the little Bushman carrying his prize. She was sure now that she had got a very good record of that hunt and her pleasure at this triumph helped a bit on the first stage of the long way back to the camp. But it was hard going. Afterwards she could hardly remember the rest of the journey. She felt confused by the shimmering waves of heat that swept over the desert. Dunes of sand seemed to stand on end in the sky. Trees had lost their roots and appeared to float above the earth. Pools of water appeared and disappeared upon the far horizon. She closed her eyes against the shafts of cruel terrifying sun as she plodded on trying to keep up with her three fellow travellers.

What was she doing here? She thought. She must have been mad to come. Tomorrow she hoped she would think it had been worthwhile, but now, with the sun beating upon her head and her feet burning so painfully that they seemed twice their usual size, she felt that all she needed was to be out of this and in some place that was shady and cool, and if she ever got to it she would never move again. She fixed her eyes on to the trail of footsteps in front of her. This way she could avoid seeing the cruel light. There was a shout from Toma and she looked up. A vehicle was coming towards them, the smaller one from the camp. Perry felt so relieved that she could have burst into tears. When it drew alongside it stopped and Fabian jumped out, followed by Samgau. She almost collapsed as he held her by the shoulders.

'Perry! Good God, girl, whatever made you do a thing like this? You must have been crazy to undertake such an expedition on your own!'

'I . . . I . . . oh, Fabian!' She wanted to cry, but the sight of his angry face prevented her. She smiled instead, trying to appear without a care in the world. 'Fabian, you will be pleased when you see the camera shots I've got. It's on ciné as well, the complete record of Toma's hunt for the springbok, and I got a shot of lions making a kill.'

'You what? Oh, Perry, you crazy girl! I don't know whether I should kiss you or kill you.' Suiting action to his words, he took her in his arms and she felt the strength and hardness of his mouth upon hers. 'You were quite determined to have your own way about Toma and Nusi, weren't you? So you send us all half mad with anxiety wondering what on earth you've got up to. I tell you Mark is biting his nails back there at the camp. I only persuaded him to stay because I wanted to have room to bring you all back.'

Why need he mention Mark now? She had forgotten all about Mark as Fabian held her in his arms. That kiss . . . it had consolidated all the feelings that she had been experiencing during the last few confusing days. Why couldn't he feel the same?

It was heavenly to have a cool shower and get into fresh clothes. Just for once to improve her morale she would wear the silk printed blouse and the blue slacks and look a little more glamorous than usual. But first she must rest; she lay in the green tent with little Topaz dozing at her side and thought about the day and the fact that she had achieved her object both about getting the film and about solving their problem for Toma and Nusi. She thought about Fabian. How angry he had looked when he had arrived to fetch them and how charming his smile had been when he had kissed her. But no more of that. She must be sensible.

'You sure had Fabian in a tizzy,' said Paul, pouring out a whisky and offering her the lounging seat that he had just vacated.

'Perhaps that was the idea,' Samantha joined in rather waspishly. 'But I thought the plan was to worry Mark, wasn't that it, Perry?'

'Hardly,' said Perry. Something, the whisky perhaps, was making her feel a bit lightheaded and she felt she did not care what catty remarks Samantha cared to make. 'My main object was to help Toma and Nusi and to take photographs of a hunt. I'm hoping I succeeded on both issues.'

'Quite the little girl scout, aren't you?' said Samantha. She was looking lovely, her honey-coloured hair coiled up on her head, her green eyes sparkling and her skin brown from the sunbathing that she indulged in very discreetly in the morning hours. Beside her Perry was conscious that her own fair skin had reddened in the fiery heat of this trying day, that in fact she felt like a boiled lobster.

'How sunburned you are,' Samantha commented.

'It was a long hot trudge back.'

'Well, if you will make a martyr of yourself, you have to put up with a bit of discomfort.'

Perry closed her eyes. She had thought the drink would make her feel relaxed, but her head was throbbing. She wished she could excuse herself, but Nusi arrived with the news that they were to have a dance to celebrate Toma's success at hunting and she did not want to let Fabian down a second time about the photography, for they were to see the ceremony of initiation whereby Toma was to become a man. Mark made her feel better when he came along beaming with his wide friendly smile.

'I call that a jolly good effort on your part, Perry. You did marvellously to keep up with Toma and Nusi. None of us could have done better. Fabian must revise his ideas about the usefulness of women on an expedition of this kind, mustn't he?'

After all this Perry forced herself to get through the evening. In any case, she thought, she felt better in the open air than in her little tent. She would be all right when she had had a good night's sleep, but first she must finish the photographic record. At the Bushman settlement that evening there was an air of excitement. Preparations for the dance were in full swing. The women had arrayed themselves in their finest ostrich egg jewellery and the shining beads glittered against their pale golden skin. Some way apart from the women sat Toma.

'Come on,' said Fabian to Perry. 'I've spoken to them about the film and they'll allow you to witness this ceremony because you were instrumental in Toma's success.'

He hurried her over to where Toma sat immobile and she just managed to adjust her camera as two of the others, Natamu and the old man, approached. They had painted their faces with a paste made from a mixture of charcoal and animal fat and looked very fierce and wild. Natamu had a knife in his hand and, as the camera whirred, he made a cut in Toma's forehead and rubbed a kind of powder into it.

'What is it?' asked Perry.

'Good girl – I was afraid you might faint. It's a powder made from the ashes of parts of the springbok mixed with leaves from a special bush. Now, they believe, Toma will be given the buck's keen eyesight, its strength and stamina to help him in his hunting. From this time he'll be regarded as a mature man.'

'And will he be able to marry Nusi?'

Fabian laughed. 'Of course that's the only thing you're worrying about, isn't it? Well, I can set your mind at rest; Samgau told me the older people have given their consent and they'll be married straight away.'

'I'm so glad,' said Perry. She felt odd as if part of her real self were not there. Fabian was real enough with his teasing grey eyes, but the kiss he had given her on her return seemed to have happened long ago. He put his arm around her as he led her back to the place where the dance was to take place.

'Poor Perry, you have had a tough day. You were quite crazy, of course. But no harm seems to have been done, except that your beautiful skin looks a little red. Remind me to give you some sunburn lotion when we get back to camp.'

She leaned against him gratefully, more compliant to his touch than she would normally have been, but when they came back to the group of people around the dancing circle he returned her to Mark, saying, 'Look after this girl, Mark. She's a little tired, but still eager to photograph the dance.'

While she was sitting beside Mark waiting for the dancing to begin, he took her hand and said, 'Perry, can you forgive me?'

'Whatever for, Mark?'

'Because we parted, because I didn't think we were suited all those years ago. I see now that you would have made any man working in the wilds an excellent wife. I was a fool. We should never have parted. You have so much pluck – I admire you tremendously.'

'Let's not talk about it now, Mark.'

He pressed her hand. 'No, not now, perhaps, but later. Now is not the time. I must see you alone as soon as possible.'

Now the dancing started. They enacted the hunt as Toma had told it to them, the springboks, the lions and even the baboons. The acting was amazingly realistic. Later they danced a story about the man who first found fire. The men danced round and round in a circle pretending they were the first Bushmen setting out into the dark world to look for it. They searched the sand, looked upwards to the moon, westwards to where the sun sets. The dance went on and on so long that their pounding feet made a furrow in the ground and some of the dancers began to fall into a trance. The steady pounding of the stamping feet felt like one beat. And in her head Perry felt this beat drumming and drumming as if a hammer were beating in the very core of her brain. 'I must get away,' she thought, but she was tied there by her wish not to show any weakness in front of Fabian. On the far horizon there were flashes of lightning and thunder rolled in the distance. At last one man walked to the fire and taking the burning coals within his grasp scattered them far and wide. The dance was over and Perry was free to go.

'Are you all right, Perry?' It was Mark beside her as they made their way back to the camp.

'Yes, why?'

'You stumbled – I thought you were going to fall.'

Perry put her hand to her aching head.

'I am tired . . . exhausted, in fact. I'll be all right after a good night's sleep.'

'Let me help you.'

He put his arm around her and she felt glad of his support. And it was like this that Fabian saw them as he came up behind, walking quickly with Samantha and Paul.

'Old acquaintance seems to be ripening,' said Samantha. 'How well did you two know each other before?'

Perry felt she could not care about any remarks Samantha chose to make. She was too weary, too grateful for Mark's supporting arm to discard it. At the moment she did not care what anyone thought of their relationship, even Fabian as he passed them with a quizzical smile.

'Can I ask Samantha to come and help you?' Mark asked as he brought her to the entrance of the tent.

'No, Mark, don't worry. I'll take a couple of aspirin. I have rather a headache – I think I was out in the sun too much today.'

Perry slept for a little while and woke feeling worse. Now she realized with a sinking heart that she was really ill. She tossed and turned, feeling the fever growing. Her head was aching so that she longed for some release from the pain. She must try to get help. But from whom? She cringed from appealing to Samantha. She would go to Mark. Her mind was too muddled to think that she should provide herself with some protection against the cool night air as she came out of the tent clad in only a thin sleeping suit and stumbled towards the truck where she knew Mark was sleeping. She was close to the fire now and although part of her felt as if she were burning up she was cold and shivering at the same time. She paused, longing for some warmth, and a figure rose beside the dying fire and came towards her.

'Perry, is anything wrong?'

His face wavered before her eyes, that face that she had seen in her dreams so often. But she must not ask help from Fabian. In her muddled half delirious state she still felt she must not show him that she had made herself ill by what he had termed her crazy behaviour. She tried to smile.

'I'm going to see Mark,' she said.

Fabian drew back and she saw the swift frown that creased his brow. 'I see. Are you in the habit of visiting Mark at this hour? It's three o'clock.'

'It doesn't matter. I don't think he'll mind what time it is.'

'I'm sure he won't, but, Perry, I didn't want it to be like this for you.'

'Like what?' She was bewildered. Her head felt as if she had an anvil inside it and someone was striking it with great slow thuds.

'I thought if you came together again it would be with marriage in mind. Don't throw yourself away, Perry, after waiting all these years. I didn't think you were the kind of woman to hold yourself cheaply. However, I expect you'll tell me it's none of my business and that it was my fault that you parted all those years ago. I suppose you feel you must make up for lost time now.'

His voice was hard and his smile sardonic. Through her hazy state of mind it penetrated that he thought she was going to Mark to make love to him. No, this was too much! She started to laugh.

'Let me share the joke. Tell me what's amusing you?' asked Fabian.

But now she had started she went on and on and found she could not stop. Great shudders shook her body as she listened to the noise that she was making that seemed to come from a stranger. Fabian strode across to her and held her to him.

'Stop that this instant, Perry! What in heaven's name is the matter with you?' She tried to struggle from his grasp, but he held her firmly, and now she found she was weeping. 'Good God, your body is on fire! You're ill, child. Why didn't you tell me? Come to the truck. I'll rouse Mark – we must do something about this immediately.'

She felt him lift her up competently and gently and she was aware of a great relief. Everything would be all right now. She could leave things to Fabian. And that was her last conscious thought.

CHAPTER ELEVEN

SHE was cool at last, cool between white sheets that smelled faintly of lemon verbena, and there was a fragrance in the room, the scent of cologne. Above her head were poles that stretched in an intricate pattern beneath a roof of thatch. Where was she, and what had happened to her little green tent? Someone was sitting at a small table, a piece of sewing in her hands, bent head covered with a white veil. Perry felt quite bewildered and yet calm and at peace.

'Hello,' she said, her voice sounding a little faint and strange to her own ears. The person at the table put down her sewing and rose in that swift uniform motion that nuns have. She had a round rosy face and blue eyes beneath the white coif.

'So,' she said with a guttural accent, 'you wake at last. You have been long time not knowing where you are.'

Perry smiled faintly. She felt peaceful and relaxed. 'I still don't know. Where am I?'

The sister came over to the bed and smoothed the coverlet that was already without a wrinkle.

'You are at Convent of Sacred Heart on banks of lake. You were brought here because Mr. Sinclair thought it dangerous to travel to Johannesburg. You were very ill and he was worried out of his wits. So good man. You are fortunate to have friend like him.'

'Yes.' Perry was drowsy. So Fabian had brought her here. She could not remember it. Perhaps later she would recall something of the trip, but not now. She felt at the moment that nothing mattered but the peaceful atmosphere of this little room.

'What is your name?' she asked the nun.

'You may call me Céleste,' said the sister, nodding her head emphatically. 'Mother Thérèse will be glad to hear you are speaking now. Each day there is a message by radio from Mr. Sinclair. Today she will have good news for him.'

Each day! Perry's heart beat a little faster and she felt such a wave of happiness flowing through her that she felt Céleste must sense her joy. But she must not think this way. Of course he felt responsible for any member of the party, and she had become very ill. It was only natural that he would try to find out how she was progressing. Tears of weakness sprang into her eyes and trickled slowly down her cheeks.

'What is this, then? We cannot have tears. You must be strong. I will go and tell Sister Dominic that you must have some chicken broth and you shall feed yourself. That will be better than a feeding cup, *nein*?'

She bustled off and was back in no time at all with a pretty tray upon which was the broth, some thin toast and wafer-thin slices of chicken. Propped up on the pillows, Perry was able to look out of the window and saw to her amazement that there was a large sheet of water nearby and growing there were red and white waterlilies. As she watched a large white bird landed in graceful flight upon the water.

'But it's all so different from the desert,' she said.

'Not always. Can be dry here too. But we have just had good rains. They start the day you came. How Mr. Sinclair must have struggled to get through to us.'

Perry remembered now the thunder and lightning in the distance.

'Did they have rain in the desert too?' she asked.

'Oh, yes, my child. And when they have rain it is as if God sent one of his miracles. Everything is, how can I say, reborn. Flowers and leaves grow where before there was plant as dead. It is a resurrection.'

And I missed it, thought Perry regretfully. She thought sadly of the people at the camp, and most of all she thought of Fabian and of what he must think of her since she had let him down and proved what he had thought all along that it had been foolish to take a woman along to do the photography. Each day she got back some of her strength. The colour returned to her face and, sitting in the peaceful garden of the convent, she regained a little of the sun tan she had lost. Although he remained in radio communication with the sisters, Fabian never once expressed a wish to speak to her and she was too shy to ask. Then, when a few days had passed and she was feeling stronger, Sister Céleste came to her and said, 'Good news. Your young man comes to fetch you tomorrow. A plane has been chartered and you will be able to go back to Johannesburg.'

How odd of Céleste to call Fabian by such a name! 'Your young man' indeed! But how good it would be to see him. The expedition must be over and they would be returning home.

She wondered how she could possibly sleep that night and decided to ask Céleste for a sleeping tablet.

'Why in the name of God do you need one of those?' asked Céleste frankly. 'You should be able to sleep well, knowing you are being fetched and going home tomorrow. Is it excitement, perhaps? Ah, well, my dear, he seems good man, very attractive. I wish you happiness and God's blessing in the future. We shall be sorry to see you go.'

In spite of the sleeping tablet she woke very early and getting up went to the window. She felt very much at peace, perhaps as the result of the night's sound rest, and the scene in front of her did nothing to detract from this. In the early morning light, pelicans were preening themselves on the still luminous water or landing feet first with a long wake of ripples. Flamingoes dug for their food in the wet sand, their curved beaks busy. Cormorants sat on stumps like something from a Japanese painting. The desert scene had been abruptly snatched from her and had been replaced by this other one, and for a few days she had been living in an atmosphere of peace and tranquillity, but she longed with painful desire to be back again in that harsh dry air, to hear the rustling of the restless wind in the golden grass and to wake in her small green tent hearing the cautious sounds of small night animals and knowing that on the morrow she would see Fabian.

Ah, but she was to see him this very day. How would he look? What would he say? Would he be annoyed that she had failed him at the last? Or would he be more gentle than usual because she had been ill? But she did not want that. She preferred to be on an equal footing. She would explain that she would do her best to develop the photographs and print them in Johnnesburg as soon as possible.

Someone must have packed her clothes, for they were all here and she changed into the printed silk blouse, for there was no need to be practical any more. In a little while they would be back in Johannesburg. During the last few days her colour had come back and she was pleased with the reflection that greeted her in the small mirror of the convent guest room. Perry sat quite still looking out of the window, unable to concentrate on the book she had picked up, only able to wonder how she would feel when she saw Fabian again. And then she heard something, the swishing sound of Sister Céleste's robes as she came down the corridor, her gruff German voice, and the answering sound of a man's voice. There was a knock at the door.

'Here she is, your invalid, but an invalid no longer, isn't it?'

'Mark!' Perry tried to look pleased to see him as he came towards her, his hands outstretched. But something in her expression must have told him that she had not expected him.

'Didn't Sister tell you I was coming to fetch you?' he asked, smiling. 'Aren't you pleased to be well enough to make the journey?'

'Oh, yes, yes, very pleased. How lovely to see you, Mark.'

She had recovered herself. He must never know how bitterly disappointed she felt that Fabian had not come. He put his arms around her and gave her a gentle kiss. Sister Céleste tactfully withdrew.

'Nice of Fabian to send me, I thought. I was very glad I could come for you. He's really a very decent sort, you know. We had a long chat and he said perhaps he'd been wrong to separate us all those years ago. He said that he'd been impressed with your behaviour on the trip and that you would have made a good wife for anyone in our profession.'

'Very good of him,' said Perry.

She went to the window and through a haze of tears saw that the pelicans and flamingoes were wheeling over the calm water, above the still reflections of the scarlet lilies, but for her the scene had lost its beauty.

'You seem a little upset. I'm sorry, I shouldn't have spoken of it so soon, but it seemed so lovely to see you again, Perry.'

Mark's frank expression was clouded as if he sensed her distress.

'Dear Mark, I'm glad to see you too.' She squeezed

his hand. 'I'm still a bit touchy. Don't take any notice of me.'

Sister Céleste came in with a tray of coffee and biscuits and their conversation turned to the journey in front of them. They were to fly straight to Johannesburg on a chartered plane. The expedition had been wound up and the rest of the party were already on their way home. Ken had recovered, but too late to rejoin them. In a few days' time Fabian would be flying to London to negotiate about the television rights. He had been in touch with Mike, Perry's partner, about developing the films in her absence. Mike had agreed to do this, so Perry need not worry about getting back to work before she was really fit again. It seemed, thought Perry, that she was not even to see Fabian again. She was not even necessary any more. Mike was quite capable of dealing with her films. He knew the camera even better than she did and from a professional point of view it hardly mattered whether he or she did the finishing work. They were both in accord about how it should be done.

As the plane gained height, she said a mental farewell to the desert. Life had been hard there and she had often been wretched, but she would not forget it easily, this golden land with its fascinating creatures.

'What's to happen to Topaz?' she asked.

'He's being sent to Johannesburg Zoo for the time being. You'll be able to see him.'

'I'm glad of that.'

But she would not be able to see Fabian. Why did she feel so wretched? She must begin to forget. It had all been a foolish illusion like the mirage of a still deep pool seen in a thirsty land. She would get over it as she had got over Mark. She glanced at the man at her side. He was a good-looking man with his air of out of doors and his clear blue eyes and deep tan, but it was incredible to remember him as the young boy on whom she had spent so much emotion years ago in another lifetime. So again she would resume her life in Johannesburg and forget this foolish passion that had arisen for Fabian in her innermost heart. But what was there left for her? She dreaded the return to a life that seemed empty now.

Mark drove her to her flat and she was glad of his company, for she was afraid to be alone with her thoughts. He stopped at a delicatessen and bought some Italian food and a bottle of red wine. The flat had been cleaned, but it seemed unlived-in and airless. Perry turned on the air-conditioner and the coolness seemed odd and artificial.

'I'd love to have a shower,' she said.

'Well, go ahead. It's your home. I'll heat up the food and set the table. I think I can find the things.'

She washed away the weariness of the journey, although she still felt very flat and depressed.

'Fabian rang while you were in the shower,' Mark informed her. 'I told him you were well. I asked him if you were to phone back, but he said not to bother. I told him we were just about to eat.'

Perry had a bitter pang of regret. The fact that Mark was there while she showered and that he was going to eat with her would have convinced Fabian of their renewed interest in each other. But what did it matter? For she knew Fabian did not care what she did. She tried to respond to Mark's kindness. What would she have done without him tonight? He was easier to talk to now that she knew him better and they enjoyed the companionable feeling of eating and the simple meal together, the lasagne, a palatable green pasta, layered with cheese sauce and savoury minced meat, the green salad accompanied by the glasses of red Chianti poured from its bottle encased in straw. Perry tried to push to the back of her mind the bitter regret that she had missed the opportunity of talking to Fabian on the phone. What could this conversation have been anyway if it were not very stilted or businesslike? He probably wanted to know about the arrangements for developing the films. Well, she would leave Mike to give him this information. She dared not risk meeting him again, feeling as she did.

'I'm sorry, I didn't hear what you were saying,' she said to Mark. She had realized he had been talking to her.

He looked a little hurt.

'I said that now I've found you again, I'm not going to let you go so easily. I expect to be in Johannesburg for a little while before going off again and I'd be glad if I could see you again. Would you like that, Perry?'

She hesitated. But why not? Mark was a dear person in spite of the fact that as far as she was concerned the magic spark that had been between them had now entirely disappeared. But she found she could not conceal a yawn.

'I'm sorry, Mark, I really am dead on my feet. I feel I want to sleep for days. But do phone before you leave. I'd like to see you again.'

He was on his feet. 'You must go to bed now. You're still far from strong. I'll ring you in the morning.' He pressed her hand as he left and kissed her gently. 'Lovely to be together again.' But she only nodded. She could not bring herself to speak.

The doctor had told her she must rest, but she could not endure the loneliness of the flat. He suggested she should go to some mountain resort, but, although she dreaded meeting him, as long as she knew Fabian was in the same city, she could not bear to leave it. During the next few days Mark phoned her regularly and she responded with more alacrity than she would have done if she had not been feeling this bitter restlessness and dissatisfaction with her life. She insisted on going to the studio and helping Mike to develop the films. Faith, Mike's wife, had recovered from her illness and they had managed to save the baby, so he was on top of the world and exultant that he was about to become a father. Perry tried to respond to his vibrant happiness, but found it difficult.

'I really don't think you should be doing any work,' Mike said to her one morning, remarking on her pallor. 'I'm afraid the desert trip was too much for you, in spite of the fact that you tell me you enjoyed it.'

'I did enjoy it. It was wonderful,' she assured him.

'And you didn't find Fabian such an ogre as you'd expected?'

'No,' she said consideringly. 'I do admit, Mike, that he's a very dedicated and clever man.'

'I knew you two would get on together once you'd met,' Mike said with satisfaction. 'Some of these photographs are terrific.'

'I'm glad you like them.'

Perry herself was very pleased with the results of her work.

'Wait until Fabian sees them. Did I tell you he phoned me to say he would come in this afternoon?'

'What a pity,' Perry said the first thing that came into her head. 'I won't be able to see him. I have a dressmaker's appointment.'

She would make this lie half true, she thought later that afternoon, by going to do some shopping. She had promised to accompany Mark to a restaurant for dinner, because it was to be his last night here for a while. She would buy a new dress and see if that would act as a tonic.

The owner of the boutique where she was known commented on her loss of weight.

'You're even more slender than you were before,' she said. 'I have a beautiful dress in gold printed silk with a halter neck. It would suit your colouring perfectly.'

'I don't know,' Perry hesitated. 'Isn't it a little daring?' The dress was beautiful but cut low at the back.

'Not at all. Remember we have the long hot summer to get through. Think how fabulous it will be to wear at the Christmas and New Year parties beside someone's swimming pool or on the patio.'

'I'll try it,' Perry decided.

Her back looked honey-gold against the rich complimenting glow of the silk, and the style and beautiful cut enhanced her slender figure.

'It's your dress. It's gorgeous,' said the saleslady.

'I'll take it,' said Perry before she had time to hesitate.

From there she went to the hairdresser's and spent a restful hour while a talkative Italian man evolved an elaborate coiffure of high-piled curls. She felt strange when she looked in the mirror, but it was all part of her plan to feel different and rid herself of the last memories of life in the wilds. She bought new make-up too, luminous honey-gold powder and an apricot-coloured stick to recompense her for her pallor.

'Wow!' breathed Mark when he came to call for her that evening. 'I'm flattered, Perry. Is this all for me?' She blushed and shook her head, but he took her hand and pressed it to his lips. 'I hardly dare touch you, you look so beautiful. I'm glad I booked a table at the Carlton – I want everyone to see what a gorgeous girl I'm taking out tonight.'

'I should have thought you would hate sophisticated

city restaurants,' she commented.

'Not a bit of it. When in Rome, you know. I have plenty of living in the wilds on my own. Tonight you can show me the town.'

Perhaps she had made a mistake to make the effort to look glamorous. She foolishly had not realized that it would give Mark the impression that she had done it for him. She had felt so tired of her old self that she had wanted to prove something, to know that she could look beautiful and well and vibrant again. But it had made Mark more amorous than he had been before. She began to dread the evening, and then shrugged off this feeling and decided she would enjoy herself and give Mark an evening to remember when he was back in the wilds.

When they arrived at the beautiful restaurant, it was crowded and the noise of the band and the chatter of the cosmopolitan crowd quite startled her, so far was it removed from the life she had grown used to during the last few weeks, but they were led to a small table in a comparatively quiet corner, far removed from the band, and the wine waiter took Mark's order for champagne cocktails while they studied the vast menu. The maître d'hôtel informed them that he had some fresh guinea-fowl and was rather startled when they laughed.

'I'm so sorry,' Perry apologized. 'We've just come from a place where we had to exist on guinea-fowl and other wild game.'

'Ah, now I understand. Then may I suggest fresh langoustines flown today from the coast, followed by river trout from the mountains cooked in wine and cream.'

'That sounds wonderful,' they agreed. And Mark ordered a bottle of Blue Nun, a Rhine wine that was delicately flavoured to match that of the langoustine and trout.

'Would you like to dance while we're waiting?' asked Mark.

'Why not?' smiled Perry. She felt in a strange mood, gay and reckless as if she had indeed cast aside that self that had given her pain during her sojourn in the desert.

Mark smiled at her as he led her on to the small dance floor.

'It's a long time since we danced together,' he said, and swept her into his arms. This was the way to forget-fulness, she assured herself, to learn to enjoy herself just for the moment as she followed the romantic beat of the music.

'Look who's here!'

A familiar voice pierced the dream world that Perry had conjured up in her mind, a world where only light and gaiety existed. Mark held her in his supporting grasp as Samantha swayed towards them, dancing with Fabian. Samantha glittered in clinging silver and the emeralds at her throat matched her eyes. She looked older, more sophisticated than the young girl who had drifted around the camp playing her guitar. And Fabian. Perry forced herself to look at him. Why, oh, why did one glimpse of his dark proud head, the aqui-line features, the piercing grey eyes and flashing smile, make nonsense of all her resolution to forget him?

'Perry and Mark too! Good to see you're enjoying yourselves together again,' he smiled at both of them impartially. 'If you would care to, join us at our table for coffee after you've dined. Paul is there and would be delighted to see you both.'

He had hardly glanced in Perry's direction. The dinner that followed was delicious, but Perry felt she might as well be eating sawdust. She laughed and joked gaily with Mark, but all the time inside her she felt a bitter hurt.

'What do you say ... shall we join them? I really don't want to give you up to other people tonight,' said Mark, pressing her hand. 'But I suppose we should, just for a little while.'

They made their way over to the other table. The three men all in dark dinner jackets looked astonishingly handsome in their various ways. Paul was very distinguished with his silver hair and worldly expression, and it was hard for Perry to think that she had last seen Fabian in shorts and safari jacket, for in his well-cut suit he looked like a city-dweller who had just come back from some holiday to account for his splendid tan. Coffee was served with delicious petits fours and fruits encased in a brittle caramel coating. Samantha was talking to Mark and presently they rose to go on to the dance floor. Someone called Fabian over to an adjacent table and Perry found herself left with Paul.

'You're looking very lovely tonight, Perry. Mark is a fortunate man.'

She shook her head, laughing, but obviously he did not take her denial seriously.

'So the ice maiden has unfrozen, or did Mark always possess your heart? I'm inclined to think so. Tonight you look so warm and glowing, absolutely beautiful.'

'Thank you, Paul, but really you only saw me at my worst, didn't you?'

'I wouldn't say that. You often looked quite beautiful in the desert. But it was only after that time when you'd gone with Fabian to fetch Mark that you became really transformed. How foolish of me to think that Fabian had anything to do with it.'

Perry thought it was just as well he believed this. He seemed normally so astute, but in this case he was on the wrong track altogether.

'We're travelling to London tomorrow,' Paul went on. 'We had hoped that Fabian would come with us, but he says he still has ends to tie up here. I'm afraid Samantha has come to the conclusion that he'll remain a loner for life. But she's not heartbroken. Certainly a more worldly kind of husband would suit her, though it wouldn't surprise me if she continues to work on Fabian when he's in London.'

'When does he expect to go?' asked Perry.

'Some time during the next few days. He was saying your pictures are quite marvellous. Apparently he saw them this afternoon, didn't he?'

'I believe so. Mike showed them to him. I wasn't there.'

'Too bad you missed the praise.'

'She hasn't missed it. It's just been a little delayed.'

Fabian stood behind her chair. He leaned down towards her and the sparkling grey eyes were very close to hers.

'You never danced when we were in the desert. But perhaps I can persuade you now.'

Before she could make any decision for herself, he had drawn her to her feet and led her on to the dance floor.

Perry had seen that he was proficient when he and Samantha danced during the expedition, but this was entirely different, much more intimate than an exhibition of skill. The small floor was crowded but dark, everyone absorbed in their own partner, and, as she was held close in his embrace, she and Fabian seemed to be in a shadowy world of their own. He was silent and she was aware that the defences she had built against emotion had crumbled at his touch. She had been pretending all evening that she did not care about him, that she could be content with a superficial world in which beautiful dresses and coiffures were the most important thing in life, a world of artificial gaiety, but when she felt his arms around her, when she looked up at him and saw the strange enigmatic expression of his grey eyes, she was appalled and yet thrilled by the passionate desire she felt to be with him always, to be part of his life for ever. But this was impossible. Why had they met this evening? It would have been better if it had not happened.

'You look very different from the small sick kitten I delivered to Sister Céleste,' he said, smiling. 'You're a radiant golden girl tonight. I was evidently well advised to send Mark to fetch you. His company has restored you, I can see that.'

Odd, thought Perry, how one can present a radiant appearance to the world while feeling that the heart is slowly dying inside one's breast. She tried to smile at him.

'I'm quite well again. I'm sorry I let you down at the end.'

'The films and stills are terrific, just what I wanted. They're going to be a great help to me. I'd no idea you were such an expert.'

'I'm pleased with them myself,' Perry admitted.

'The shots of the hunt with Toma and Nusi are particularly good because they were such a good-looking couple. It was a pity the consequences were so drastic for you.'

The music was drawing to a close and the seconds of time in which she could be alone with him were almost ended. And here they were talking about things that were no longer significant. Of course she was pleased that the pictures were a success, but what did they matter compared with the fact that soon Fabian would be gone and she would most probably never see him again?

'Why the sad expression, Perry? Is it because you're not dancing with Mark?'

She looked at him, unable to speak. How bitterly she regretted now that she had told him of her previous attachment. From then he had concluded that she still harboured romantic feelings for Mark.

'Tonight you certainly don't look like a suitable future wife for a wild life authority,' he went on. 'It's hard to remember the Perry we knew in camp. What have you done with those khaki slacks that you hated so much?'

He was laughing down at her with his faunlike mocking smile.

'I've given them to my washwoman's son,' she declared defiantly. 'He can find more use for them than I can. I don't expect to be in the desert for a long while, if ever, in the future.'

'What will you do? Go back to photographing fashion models?'

'I expect so.'

The music had stopped and they made their way back to the table. Mark rose eagerly as they approached.

'It's time to get you home, Perry. She looks glowingly healthy, doesn't she?' he asked the others. 'But she tires easily. I have to look after her.'

Why did he have to assume this possessive air in front of Fabian? Perry thought desperately. Everything seemed to confirm his opinion that they had come together again.

She was quiet as they drove home in the car that Mark had hired for his stay in the city.

'Has it been too much for you tonight?' Mark took his hand from the wheel and pressed her hand.

'I am a little weary,' she admitted. 'I'm sorry, Mark, since it's your last evening here.'

'There'll be more evenings. Now we've come together again, I don't mean to lose you so easily.'

In spite of her tiredness, she felt she must find some way to discourage him. It was unfair to start this all over again when she knew she was incapable of loving him. She let him come up to the flat, searching in her mind what to say. But as soon as they were inside the door she found herself in his arms, and he was kissing her as if he would make up for all the missing years between. She pushed him gently away.

'No, Mark, I'm sorry.'

'I'm sorry too, Perry. I've been longing for that all evening, but I should have remembered that you've been ill and tonight has been too hectic for you.'

'Oh, Mark, it isn't only that. Come and sit down.'

She led him to the curved couch that overlooked the fabulous view of the city. Cars were still forming a long glittering snake of light along the distant freeway.

'Mark, I've been wrong to take advantage of your friendship.'

'What do you mean, Perry? I'd hoped it was more than friendship. Hasn't it been wonderful to meet again?'

'Yes, it has. Of course it has. But, Mark, our time for loving has passed. We can never feel the same again.'

'You really think that? We could give it a try. You could grow to love me again.'

'No, Mark, I'm sorry.'

His blue eyes were hurt and troubled.

'Tell me the truth, Perry. Is there someone else?'

She got up from the couch and looked out of the window at the glittering lights, then turned to face him. If she was to be fair, she must admit it.

'Yes, Mark. I am in love with someone, but it's hopeless.'

'Is he married?'

'No, he's just not the marrying kind.'

'Oh, one of those. There are plenty of his type in a city like this, I suppose. Take care, Perry, you're worth more than that.'

'Oh, Mark, it's not like that at all. He doesn't think of me in that way. When he leaves Johannesburg, as he will do soon, he'll forget that I ever existed.'

'Then he must be as crazy as I was to throw away your love. But I had the excuse of youth. Well, Perry, I'll keep in touch with you and go on hoping.'

She kissed him gently.

'Dear Mark, it's no use.'

CHAPTER TWELVE

PERRY awoke next morning feeling drained and exhausted. When she looked over the city, there was a stillness about the air and an ominous electric feeling as if, still far away but coming nearer to invade the bright blue firmament, a storm were brewing. This was the time of year in Johannesburg when sharp storms struck suddenly in the afternoon, heralded by intense heat and the gradual piling up of cumulus clouds on the horizon. She put on a sleeveless sheath of a dress in tobacco brown shantung and topped it with a three-quarter length raincoat of buttercup yellow. Her red-gold hair was coiled in a knot at the back of her head, for she had brushed out the elaborate style, and she wore a gold bracelet in a modern design of roughly wrought gold.

This morning she felt too weary to cope with the traffic, so decided to take the bus and sat in a dream as it passed the blocks of smart flats and sunlit gardens. Sometimes when the view opened out a little there were splashes of yellow cassia trees and jacarandas of misty purple. Spring had come to Johannesburg while she had been away in the desert. Men were wearing their lightweight summer suits and young girls were in new flick skirts and striped sleeveless tops. Perry saw a man and a girl, lingering at a corner, reluctant to part and go on their way to work, obviously enthralled with each other's company. She felt a twist of envy. How lovely it must be to be able to acknowledge your love to each other and not have to repress it.

But she must not think of that, for last night she had made a resolve that she would try to put love out of her life and start thinking about her work here in Johannesburg and not cast her mind back to the events during the expedition. But that was rather difficult, because as she opened the door of the studio Mike said, 'Surprise, surprise!' and on the large stand that they usually used for exhibitions were all the best shots of the Kalahari, including a large picture of Fabian holding Topaz in his arms and with his characteristic smile. Another one in more serious mood showed him talking to Natamu. Perry wished with all her heart that Mike had not done this. Of course he expected her to be pleased and thrilled and she had to try to pretend that she was, when all the time the sight of Fabian, so lively and so real, depressed her still more.

'Fabian was quite ecstatic about the photographs,' Mike informed her jubilantly. 'It was great of you, Perry, to make such a fine job of it. Now, when he organizes something else, he's bound to ask you.'

'Heaven forbid!' It had slipped out before Perry could stop it.

Mike frowned. 'Why do you say that? I thought you two got on well together. I don't blame you, though. It must have been pretty rough. Anyhow, I'm hoping I shall be able to go next time. He's proposing to investigate eagles in the Drakensberg, and that wouldn't be so bad because Faith could come too and stay at a hotel. You could come to keep her company.'

'And who would look after the studio?'

'I'm thinking of getting a young assistant. I have one in mind. But this is all in the future. Fabian was a little vague about his plans.'

That was just as well, thought Perry. Nothing would induce her to join this expedition. But she could make a stand when the time came. She threw herself into the work of printing some shots of African mine dancers that had been ordered and was so busy all morning that she did not have time to be depressed. Mike had a lunch date with a client, but she sent out for a sandwich and milk shake from a nearby café. As she ate she could not resist having another look at the screen full of Kalahari photographs and she had such a yearning for the desert that she felt she could not bear it. What could she do about it? Her eyes fell on the pictures of Topaz. That was it. It was foolish, maybe sentimental, but she would go to see the little creature this afternoon as soon as she had finished work.

She asked Mike rather apologetically if she could leave a little earlier than usual as she had decided to go to Zoo Lake to see Topaz.

'Of course, it's all right as far as I'm concerned, but you may get wet. There's a storm brewing. Have you seen the cumulus clouds outside?'

'I have a raincoat,' said Perry, 'and the bus stops at the gates.'

'Haven't you got your car?'

'No, but it doesn't matter.'

After life in the desert, thought Perry, a small Johannesburg storm could hardly affect her, and in any case it often came to nothing. As she came into the street, clouds were towering in mountainous formations over the city that seemed torpid in the heat of the afternoon. The bus passed the mansions of the rich, white-painted villas with gardens ablaze with colour, and swimming pools surrounded by bright patio furniture. As she descended and made her way in to the park-like surroundings of the zoo, thunder rumbled in the distance and the sun disappeared. But she could shelter here if the need arose. She made inquiries about Topaz and a friendly keeper led her to a secluded part of the grounds.

'We haven't put him on show to the public yet, miss, because Mr. Sinclair didn't want it. He said he hadn't decided what to do with the little cub. He was wondering whether he could be returned to a game reserve when he was old enough to fend for himself, so he doesn't want him to get used to people too much. It's a bit of a problem.'

'Has he been to see him, then?' Perry could not resist asking.

'Yes, quite a few times. The little cub is very tame with him.'

And here he was, Topaz with his tawny fluffy coat still spotted on the underside, peering out of the shelter in his cage; evidently he had been asleep and was now a little startled by the noise of the thunder.

'Can I hold him?' asked Perry.

The keeper looked doubtful. 'He has very sharp claws already, miss. I'd better hold him first.'

But when Topaz was in the keeper's arms he mewed at Perry. It was quite clear that he still knew her. She took him in her arms, handling him as she had become used to doing. He had grown quite a bit in these few weeks, but he was still gentle, fluffy and lovable. His eyes blinked sleepily at her and his paws were soft as silk.

'Oh, what a gorgeous wee thing you are,' she said.

'He is,' said the keeper. 'Whoever had the upbringing of him in the desert looked after him very well. He's a fine specimen.'

'This young lady had a lot to do with it,' said the voice of Fabian. 'Good afternoon, Perry, fancy meeting you here.'

He had approached so silently that neither of them, absorbed as they were with Topaz, had heard him. Perry gave Topaz back into the keeper's arms and tried to speak coolly, though her heart was pounding.

'Hello, Fabian, I didn't expect to see you either. Topaz is looking well, isn't he? I'm thrilled that he still knows me after all this time.'

There was a loud roll of thunder and several spots of rain the size of silver pieces splashed upon the hot ground.

'The rain is coming,' said Perry, glad of an excuse to get away. 'I shall have to run for the bus.'

'Nonsense, I'll give you a lift.'

He helped her into her yellow raincoat, then seized her around the waist and they ran in the increasing downpour to the place where he had parked his Alfa-Romeo. Now there was no avoiding the intimacy of the closed car as the rain poured across the windscreen, blinding the occupants to anything that was happening in the outside world.

'I think we'll sit for a while,' said Fabian, 'or are you scared of the storm?'

It was not the storm that scared her, thought Perry, it was the fact that she was alone once more with Fabian and she must try not to betray by the smallest gesture or expression how much he meant to her.

'No,' she said in a small voice. 'Not at all.'

He laughed and held her firmly, his arm around her.

'You can't deceive me. You're trembling. Come on, I'll get you home if you will direct me. I can see you'll be happier under a roof.'

Wide rivulets of water were pouring across the sidewalks, but Fabian drove steadily along in the almost deserted streets, skilfully pulling the car gently over when it was inclined to skid. By the time they had reached Perry's apartment house the rain had stopped its first torrential downpour, but threatening rolls of thunder overhead showed that the storm had not yet exhausted its fury.

'I hope I'm going to be asked in for a drink,' said Fabian, opening the door on her side. 'Otherwise I'm going to die of pneumonia.'

His smile was at its most charming. How could she dismiss him? she thought in despair.

'Of course you must come in for a quick drink. I'm afraid I have a dinner date for this evening,' she lied.

'So soon after Mark's departure? Poor Mark!'

He was grinning now as if he did not believe her, but she made no reply.

'Very grand,' he said, his eyes sweeping over the gold and blue Persian rugs, the comfortable cream tweed chairs and the few carefully chosen pieces of Georgian furniture. 'It must have been a shock to your system to come with the expedition.'

'Of course it wasn't,' she said crossly. 'What about Paul and Samantha and their comforts?'

'That was catered for,' he seemed a little surprised at her vehemence, 'but you had to put up with a small tent and a lot more discomfort than Samantha did.'

Perry was cross and distraught now.

'I didn't put up with it! How can you say such a thing? I loved it. It was like a home to me, that dear little green tent. If you knew how I longed to be back in it, when I was at the mission hospital . . . but what's the use of talking to you? You just never understand how marvellous it all seemed to me. It was one of the most wonderful times of my life, perhaps the most wonderful.'

She walked across to the windows where the hand-woven cream mohair curtains were still not drawn and there was a magnificent panorama of the storm-lashed sky. She did not want him to see that she had tears in her eyes, that even now they were spilling down her cheeks. But he came behind her.

'Come away from the window, Perry. I'll draw the curtains. I thought you were afraid of storms.'

A jagged multiple flash of lightning rent the dark cobalt sky followed by a rending crash of thunder overhead.

'No, leave the curtains. I love to watch a storm.'

'So. You're not trembling because you're afraid of the storm, Perry. What is it that's scaring you?'

'Nothing,' she gulped. 'Leave me alone, I'm quite all right.'

'And that's rain on your face, I suppose, not tears? Oh, Perry darling, sweet Perry, what game are you playing with me?'

'No game,' she sniffed. She was in his arms and he was wiping the tears away. What had he called her? She must have mistaken the words.

'Do you remember the day Nusi gave you the magic bow of love?' he asked. 'I hoped then that I would be the one, but then you'd told me about Mark and I thought you cared for him.'

Perry shook her head. 'That was all over long ago. Last night I told him it was no use.'

'So he told me when I met him at the airport this morning. He said you loved someone else. Perry, it was like one of those flashes of lightning. I rushed to the studio and Mike told me I'd just missed you.'

'Then it was not a coincidence that you came to see Topaz?'

'Of course not, my sweet love. I grew to love you more and more when we were in the desert. When you were so ill, I realized that I couldn't live without you. But there was Mark. The shadow of your old love lay between us, the bitterness you'd felt towards me.'

'And now there's no more bitterness,' Perry said, putting her arms around him and lifting up her face for his kiss. 'Only love, Fabian, a love that will last a lifetime.'

THE OMNIBUS
Has Arrived!

A GREAT NEW IDEA
From HARLEQUIN

OMNIBUS — The 3 in 1 HARLEQUIN
only $1.50 per volume

Here is a great new exciting idea from Harlequin. THREE GREAT ROMANCES — complete and unabridged — BY THE SAME AUTHOR — in one deluxe paperback volume — for the unbelievably low price of only $1.50 per volume.

We have chosen some of the finest works of four world-famous authors . . .

VIOLET WINSPEAR
ISOBEL CHACE
JOYCE DINGWELL
SUSAN BARRIE

. . . and reprinted them in the 3 in 1 Omnibus. Almost 600 pages of pure entertainment for just $1.50 each. A TRULY "JUMBO" READ!

These four Harlequin Omnibus volumes are now available. The following pages list the exciting novels by each author.

Climb aboard the Harlequin Omnibus now! The coupon below is provided for your convenience in ordering.

Violet Winspear
Omnibus

"To be able to reproduce the warmly exciting world of romance . . . a colourful means of escape", this was the ambition of the young VIOLET WINSPEAR, now a world famous author. Here, we offer three moving stories in which she has well and truly achieved this.

. . . . CONTAINING

PALACE OF THE PEACOCKS . . . where we join young Temple Lane, in the ridiculous predicament of masquerading as a youth on an old tub of a steamer, somewhere in the Java Seas. She had saved for five years to join her fiancee in this exotic world of blue skies and peacock waters — and now . . . she must escape him . . . (#1318).

BELOVED TYRANT . . . takes us to Monterey, where high mountainous country is alive with scents and bird-song above the dark blue surge of the Pacific Ocean. Here, we meet Lyn Gilmore, Governess at the Hacienda Rosa, where she falls victim to the tyranny of the ruthless, savagely handsome, Rick Corderas . . . (#1032).

COURT OF THE VEILS . . . is set in a lush plantation on the edge of the Sahara Desert, where Roslyn Brant faces great emotional conflict, for not only has she lost all recollection of her fiancee and her past, but the ruthless Duane Hunter refuses to believe that she ever was engaged to marry his handsome cousin . . . (#1267).

$1.50 per volume

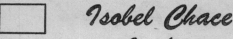

Isobel Chace
Omnibus

A writer of romance is a weaver of dreams. This is true of ISOBEL CHACE, and her many thousands of ardent readers can attest to this. All of her eagerly anticipated works are so carefully spun, blending the mystery and the beauty of love.

. . . . CONTAINING

A HANDFUL OF SILVER . . . set in the exciting city of Rio de Janeiro, with its endless beaches and tall skyscraper hotels, and where a battle of wits is being waged between Madeleine Delahaye, Pilar Fernandez the lovely but jealous fiancee of her childhood friend, and her handsome, treacherous cousin — the strange Luis da Maestro . . . (#1306).

THE SAFFRON SKY . . . takes us to a tiny village skirting the exotic Bangkok, Siam, bathed constantly in glorious sunshine, where at night the sky changes to an enchanting saffron colour. The small nervous Myfanwy Jones realizes her most cherished dream, adventure and romance in a far off land. In Siam, two handsome men are determined to marry her — but, they both have the same mysterious reason . . . (#1250).

THE DAMASK ROSE . . . in Damascus, the original Garden of Eden, we are drenched in the heady atmosphere of exotic perfumes, when Vickie Tremaine flies from London to work for Perfumes of Damascus and meets Adam Templeton, fiancee of the young rebellious Miriam, and alas as the weeks pass, Vickie only becomes more attracted to this your Englishman with the steel-like personality . . . (#1334).

$1.50 per volume

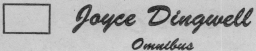

Joyce Dingwell
Omnibus

JOYCE DINGWELL'S lighthearted style of writing and her delightful characters are well loved by a great many readers all over the world. An author with the unusual combination of compassion and vitality which she generously shares with the reader, in all of her books.

. . . . CONTAINING

THE FEEL OF SILK . . . Faith Blake, a young Australian nurse becomes stranded in the Orient and is very kindly offered the position of nursing the young niece of the Marques Jacinto de Velira. But, as Faith and a young doctor become closer together, the Marques begins to take an unusual interest in Faith's private life . . . (#1342).

A TASTE FOR LOVE . . . here we join Gina Lake, at Bancroft Bequest, a remote children's home at Orange Hills, Australia, just as she is nearing the end of what has been a very long "engagement" to Tony Mallory, who seems in no hurry to marry. The new superintendent, Miles Fairland however, feels quite differently as Gina is about to discover . . . (#1229).

WILL YOU SURRENDER . . . at Galdang Academy for boys, "The College By The Sea", perched on the cliff edge of an Australian headland, young Gerry Prosset faces grave disappointment when her father is passed over and young Damien Manning becomes the new Headmaster. Here we learn of her bitter resentment toward this young man — and moreso, the woman who comes to visit him . . . (#1179).

$1.50 per volume

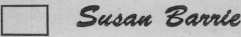

Susan Barrie
Omnibus

The charming, unmistakable works of SUSAN
BARRIE, one of the top romance authors, have
won her a reward of endless readers who take the
greatest of pleasure from her inspiring stories,
always told with the most enchanting locations.

. . . . CONTAINING

MARRY A STRANGER . . . Doctor Martin Guelder
sought only a housekeeper and hostess for his
home, Fountains Court, in the village of Herford-
shire in the beautiful English countryside. Young
Stacey Brent accepts his proposal, but soon finds
herself falling deeply in love with him — and she
cannot let him know . . . (#1043).

THE MARRIAGE WHEEL . . . at Farthing Hall, a
delightful old home nestled in the quiet countryside of Gloucestershire, we meet Frederica Wells,
chauffeur to Lady Allerdale. In need of more
financial security, Frederica takes a second post,
to work for Mr. Humphrey Lestrode, an exacting
and shrewd businessman. Almost immediately —
she regrets it . . . (#1311).

ROSE IN THE BUD . . . Venice, city of romantic
palaces, glimmering lanterns and a thousand
waterways. In the midst of all this beauty,
Catherine Brown is in search of the truth about
the mysterious disappearance of her step-sister.
Her only clue is a portrait of the girl, which she
finds in the studio of the irresistably attractive
Edouard Moroc — could it be that he knows of
her whereabouts? . . . (#1168).

$1.50 per volume